DISRUPTIVE FORCE

New York Times Bestselling Author
ELLE JAMES

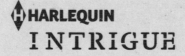

I dedicate this book to my three children, who are now grown and successful adults; to my husband, who supports my crazy habit of writing books; to my mother, who has encouraged me from the beginning; to my sister, who started this journey with me; and to my father, who taught me the value of hard work and perseverance. Family is everything and I love all of them dearly.

I miss you, Dad.

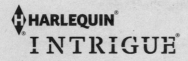

HARLEQUIN®
INTRIGUE®

ISBN-13: 978-1-335-13628-2

Disruptive Force

Copyright © 2020 by Mary Jernigan

This edition published by arrangement with Harlequin Books S.A.

For questions and comments about the quality of this book, please contact us at CustomerService@Harlequin.com.

Harlequin Enterprises ULC
22 Adelaide St. West, 40th Floor
Toronto, Ontario M5H 4E3, Canada
www.Harlequin.com

Printed in U.S.A.

Recycling programs for this product may not exist in your area.

Elle James, a *New York Times* bestselling author, started writing when her sister challenged her to write a romance novel. She has managed a full-time job and raised three wonderful children, and she and her husband even tried ranching exotic birds (ostriches, emus and rheas). Ask her, and she'll tell you what it's like to go toe-to-toe with an angry 350-pound bird! Elle loves to hear from fans at ellejames@earthlink.net or ellejames.com.

Books by Elle James

Harlequin Intrigue

Declan's Defenders

Marine Force Recon
Show of Force
Full Force
Driving Force
Tactical Force
Disruptive Force

Mission: Six

One Intrepid SEAL
Two Dauntless Hearts
Three Courageous Words
Four Relentless Days
Five Ways to Surrender
Six Minutes to Midnight

Ballistic Cowboys

Hot Combat
Hot Target
Hot Zone
Hot Velocity

SEAL of My Own

Navy SEAL Survival
Navy SEAL Captive
Navy SEAL to Die For
Navy SEAL Six Pack

Visit the Author Profile page at Harlequin.com.

CAST OF CHARACTERS

Cole McCastlain—Former Force Recon marine dishonorably discharged from the military; good with computers.

CJ Grainger—Trained to be an assassin by a secret organization called Trinity. She wants to stop Trinity from turning children into weapons.

Charlotte "Charlie" Halverson—Rich widow of a highly prominent billionaire philanthropist. Leading the fight for right by funding Declan's Defenders.

Gordon Helms—Vice president of the United States.

Chris Carpenter—Homeland Security Advisor to the president.

Roger Arnold—Charlie Halverson's butler and former UK SAS soldier.

Mack Balkman—Former Force Recon marine, assistant team leader and Declan's right-hand man. Grew up on a farm and knows hard work won't kill you—guns will.

Declan O'Neill—Highly trained Force Recon marine who made a decision that cost him his career in the Marine Corps. Dishonorably discharged from the military, he's forging his own path with the help of a wealthy benefactor.

Frank "Mustang" Ford—Former Force Recon marine, point man. First into dangerous situations, making him the eyes and ears of the team.

Augustus "Gus" Walsh—Former Force Recon marine radio operator; good with weapons, electronics and technical equipment.

Jack Snow—Former Force Recon marine slack man, youngest member of the team, takes all the heavy stuff. Not afraid of hard, physical work.

Chapter One

Are you still assigned to help me? CJ Grainger hesitated before she sent the text to Cole McCastlain.
The former member of Marine Force Reconnaissance now worked for Declan's Defenders, the
small but dedicated agency created to help fight
for justice when the police, FBI and CIA couldn't
get the job done.

A week ago, CJ had helped Declan's Defenders
by providing them information she'd found on the
dark web about a potential assault on the National
Security Council meeting.

That attack had gone down as predicted. The
VP and Anne Bellamy, a mid-level staffer for the
National Security Advisor, had been taken hostage, amid another plot involving a deadly serum.
Fortunately, Declan's team had been ready. They'd
rescued the vice president and the staffer, killed
two Trinity sleeper agents embedded within the

White House staff as well as two other agents who'd worked with them to abduct the hostages.

Trinity.

Even the thought of the name and organization made CJ break out in a sweat. She'd spent the past year hiding in plain sight. One of very few who'd escaped Trinity and lived.

I'm here, Cole texted.

Again, CJ hesitated. On her own for so long, she'd survived because of her independence and ability to disguise herself. She'd been very careful not to leave a trail a trained hacker, private investigator or Trinity-trained assassin could follow. And she didn't have anyone to be used as leverage. No Achilles' heel, no loved one Trinity could hold hostage to get her to come out into the open.

The part about no loved ones had been one of the reasons she'd been recruited into the Trinity training program in the first place. And by "recruited," she meant stolen out of a foster care home she'd been placed in by Virginia State Social Services.

The state of Virginia hadn't spent a lot of time and resources looking for a child nobody wanted.

Years ago, as a young adolescent, she'd been assimilated, brainwashed and forced to learn how to fight, how to defend herself and how to kill people Trinity ordered her to eliminate.

Until one year ago.

They'd ordered her to kill a pregnant woman. The wife of a senator. When CJ had sighted her rifle on the woman, who'd been probably eight and a half months along in her pregnancy, she hadn't been able to pull the trigger. She'd hesitated, wondering if the baby was a boy or girl and thinking that if she killed the child's mother, she'd be without a parent. And knowing that if Trinity decided the father was of no further use to them or was a risk who could expose someone within the organization, the father would be eliminated, as well. That would leave the child parentless.

Having been parentless, CJ had refused to let that happen to the unborn child.

Her hesitation hadn't helped the woman. Trinity had a second assassin waiting on a rooftop to do the job if CJ wouldn't.

The shot was fired, the bullet piercing the woman's belly, killing the baby instantly. It wasn't until much later that CJ learned the mother had died in transit to the hospital.

After she'd failed to take the kill shot, CJ had known what would happen next. Since most Trinity agents didn't get second chances if they failed an assignment, she knew the man who'd assassinated the pregnant woman and her baby would be turning his rifle on her.

CJ, anticipating the inevitable, had ducked low, out of the sight line of the rooftop from where the gunman leveled his sniper rifle and pulled the trigger.

The bullets flew well over her head. She'd tucked her rifle into the golf bag she'd carried up to the rooftop and then crawled to the door and descended to the first floor. There, she hid her golf bag under the last step of the staircase, planning to retrieve it after the furor died down.

In the meantime, she'd pulled a hooded jacket out of her satchel and slipped it on over her sweater. The added bulk made her appear heavier. She slipped on a pair of black-rimmed plastic glasses and tucked her hair under the hood of the jacket. Then she jammed her hands into the pockets of her jeans and hunched her shoulders like a teen trying to be invisible. Slipping out of the apartment building, she'd blended into the rush of people heading home from work.

Instead of going to her apartment, she'd kept walking. Nothing in that apartment meant anything to her. It had been a place to sleep and shower. She always carried everything she needed in the satchel she'd slung over her shoulder. A laptop, a couple changes of clothes, three wigs in varying colors, makeup and her Glock 9mm pistol. She'd also had a burner phone in her pocket, along with a wad of cash and a couple of credit cards that would have to be shredded since she'd become a target for the same organization she'd worked for.

For the past year, she'd been on the run, dodging shadows and living from day to day looking over her shoulder.

Are you in trouble? Cole's second message brought CJ back from her memories to the task at hand.

Are you still digging into Trinity conspirators? she texted.

CJ didn't want help, but she had to find the leader of Trinity before he found her. Two or three people searching the internet was better than one person using borrowed internet from public libraries.

Yes.

Look into Chris Carpenter, the Homeland Security Advisor for the National Security Council.

Cole's response was quick.

Got anything to go on? Any clues?

CJ hated to say she had a gut feeling about the man. A trained assassin relied on cold, hard facts, disregarding emotion and luck.

Prior to the attack in the NSC, the conference room coordinator received a text from Carpenter.

The guy who helped kidnap Anne Bellamy and the vice president?

Yes.

His assistant, Dr. Saunders, was the woman who was almost killed in a hit-and-run accident, wasn't she?

That's the one.

On it.

CJ had been doing her own digging on the dark web via the Arlington Public Library. She'd hacked in, making it past the firewall of the phone system used by Chris Carpenter to his billing information. She'd narrowed her search of his calls to the day of the attack. She'd gone through his phone records, searching for a connection to Terrence Tully, the conference room coordinator for the NSC meeting, and found one.

Terrence Tully had been one of Trinity's sleeper agents, embedded in the White House, waiting for his call to serve.

That day, he'd helped orchestrate the kidnapping of the VP and Anne Bellamy, the woman CJ had contacted to warn about the attack.

Can we meet? Cole asked.

CJ frowned. Any contact she had with others

put them at risk. She'd already broken the first rule she'd made for herself upon her defection from Trinity: stay away from anyone or anything to do with the organization. Including people who were actively searching to destroy it.

She'd broken that rule by contacting Anne to warn her of the attack.

Then she'd involved herself in Declan's Defenders' rescue effort. If that wasn't bad enough, she'd gone to their base location at Charlotte Halverson's estate. The Defenders knew more about her than she'd wanted to divulge, including what she looked like. And they'd assigned one of Declan's men to be her protector and backup.

CJ snorted. Like she'd let that happen. If she allowed anyone to get that close to her, it would be one more way for Trinity to find her and the agent would be collateral damage when Trinity came to kill her.

Being a loner was better for all involved.

She typed, If I need you, I'll find you.

CJ backed out of Carpenter's phone records she'd been perusing and went back on the dark web, digging into anything she could find that might lead her to Trinity's leader, the best kept secret in the entire organization.

When she'd first left Trinity, her main focus had been on staying alive and out of their way. It didn't take her long to realize, however, that she'd never be truly safe until the organization was destroyed. And the best way to do that was to find its leader and destroy him. Because of the recent Trinity activity in the DC area and the fact that it was a world capital, she felt confident that Trinity's head was somewhere in the vicinity.

A little more than a week ago, she'd found a particular website with a forum where anyone could anonymously arrange to hire a hit man. It seemed assassins for hire didn't like that Trinity was an exclusive organization they couldn't crack. Some of the people on the site had it out for Trinity and had made it a personal challenge to identify its leadership and/or to sabotage the organization's hits. It was on that site through online chats and more that CJ had learned about the potential attack on the White House during the NSC meeting.

Going to the site, CJ went directly to the message board.

Still looking for the Director, she typed.

A few seconds later she received this response: They're still looking for you.

Weary of the chase, the worry and living below the radar, she wrote, Time to stop T.

The time will come. We will find the Director.

Today?

Probably not.

The next message made her pulse pound.

Someone knows where you are.

CJ frowned.

How do you know?

Message traffic on another site, listing IP address of Arlington library.

She glanced out the glass window of the computer room to the library beyond. Moms were helping their children carry stacks of books to the counter, and a college student with a backpack leaned over the desk to ask the librarian a question. No one looked like a Trinity assassin. But then, she had been one and had been trained to blend in.

Where are you seeing this? she typed.

No time.

He's here now?

Now. Run. Don't go home. Compromised.

CJ cleared the browser, cleared the screen and logged off the computer. She ducked low, pretending to get something from her backpack. Instead of putting something in, she took out the blond wig cut in a short bob, pulled it on and quickly stuffed her own auburn hair beneath it. Then she took off her black leather jacket and crammed it into the backpack, straightening her pale pink T-shirt with the cartoon kitty on the front. Setting a pair of round sunglasses on her nose to hide her green eyes and popping a piece of bubble gum into her mouth, she stood.

Disguise in place, CJ exited the room through the opposite door from where she'd entered and slipped through the stacks, weaving her way along the travel section into the how-to books.

A gray-haired man peered at a gardening book for beginners. A young woman perused a book on designing websites.

CJ moved past them. She'd have to go through the front entrance to get out without setting off any emergency exit alarms.

A group of two women and six children ranging in ages from five to fourteen loaded books into bags and headed toward the door.

The college student stood at the magazine display, leafing through the tabloids.

CJ crossed the open space in front of the checkout desk and trailed the group of women and children out of the building and into the parking lot.

She looked around, keeping the door to the library in her peripheral vision.

CJ moved across the parking lot in the opposite direction of the children, not wanting them to be collateral damage should the situation get sticky. She kept walking, figuring the farther away from the library she got, the better. Once she knew she'd shaken whoever might be after her, she'd hop on a bus and head for...

Hell if she knew. If the apartment she'd rented had been compromised, she couldn't go back there.

Footsteps sounded on the pavement behind her.

CJ stepped around a large SUV and chanced a look back.

The college student had followed her out of the library. He had slipped his backpack off his shoulder and was reaching inside.

CJ made it to the sidewalk, quickly passing shops and other buildings until she found the right one. She ducked into the restaurant and walked to the back. The dim lighting forced her to remove the sunglasses. Following a waitress, she entered the kitchen.

"Sorry, miss, you can't be here," the waitress said.

CJ grimaced and glanced over her shoulder. "Is there a rear exit through here?"

"Yes, but for employees only."

"My ex-boyfriend is following me. He won't leave me alone. And he's abusive." CJ touched the waitress's arm. "Please. I need to get away from him."

The woman's eyes rounded and she looked through the glass window of the swinging door. "Dark hair and backpack?"

CJ nodded. "Yes."

The waitress grabbed her arm. "Come with me." She led CJ to the back door and out into the alley. "My husband is waiting for my shift to end. He can take you where you need to go, as long as it's not too far." She glanced down at her watch. "I get off in fifteen minutes." She took CJ's hand and led her to an older model sedan with a faded paint job.

The man in the driver's seat was asleep, his head tilted back against the headrest.

The woman tapped on the window.

Jerking awake, the man sat up and rolled down the window. "Hey, Bea, are you off already?"

"No," Bea said. "But I want you to help this woman get away from an abusive ex-boyfriend. Take her where she needs to go. I'll be ready to go when you get back."

She turned to CJ. "Ronnie will take care of you. He's a good guy, my man is." Bea opened the back door and held it for CJ. "Hurry, before he figures out which way you went."

CJ nodded, hating that she'd lied, but needing to get away. "Thank you." She climbed in and hunkered low on the backseat while Ronnie drove away from the restaurant and out onto the busy street in front.

CJ waited until they were half a block away before she looked up over the back of the seat in time to see the college student run out of the restaurant and look both directions.

When he turned and walked toward the library, CJ let out a sigh.

"Was that the guy?" Ronnie asked.

CJ nodded. "He just won't let go." Which was true. Trinity assassins were trained to keep after their target until the target had been eliminated. He'd find her again. And when he did, he wouldn't let her slip away a second time.

CJ had Ronnie drop her off at a metro station two miles from the library. She slipped onto the train headed for a neighborhood she'd been through several times. The one where Cole McCastlain lived. She wasn't ready to admit she needed help, but she'd found a furnished town house for rent near his. If it was still available, she'd crash there and regroup. She needed time to think about her next move. Maybe it was time to openly join forces with Declan's Defenders. They were all after the same thing. To bring an end to Trinity. To do so, they had to bring down the Director.

COLE SAT AT his desk in the town house he'd rented, his body tense, his gaze glued to the computer. He'd seen the messages come across the website he'd been following. He'd known Trinity was closing in on CJ. And he'd been unable to do anything but warn her. Frustration was too weak a description of what he was feeling. Cole needed action.

But CJ had refused to let him or anyone else from Declan's Defenders overtly assist her in their mutual objective to bring down Trinity. She'd insisted she was better off alone.

He'd been lucky today. The messages had come in just in time for him to warn CJ to get out of the Arlington library. Hell, he'd been able to locate her based on the IP address of the computer she'd logged in on. She'd been perusing the internet on sites known for helping people find assassins for hire. What scared him was that if he was able to find her, others could easily do the same.

He'd invested in a burner phone. Next time she texted, he'd give her that number and insist she use it with a new burner number. Trinity had to know Declan's Defenders were out to destroy the organization that had most likely put out a hit on John Halverson. Declan's Defenders would not exist but for the trust and generosity of Halverson's widow, Charlotte—Charlie.

John Halverson had been on a mission to stop Trinity's illicit activities. He'd scratched the surface and had probably gotten too close to finding their leader, thus making them desperate enough to eliminate the threat.

As much as Charlie had done for Declan and his band of former Marine Force Reconnaissance men, they wanted to return the favor. Their mission was to find the leader of Trinity, the Director. The theory was to chop off the head of the snake and the rest of the organization would die.

According to Halverson's records, he'd been searching for the same thing. It had taken him years to get as far as he had, and yet, he'd not found the Director or, at least, not been able to identify him before he was murdered.

Cole had been working with Jonah Spradlin, Charlie's computer guy. They'd been hacking into the computer system at the White House to deep dive existing background checks on people who worked there ever since CJ had given them the heads-up on a planned assault on the NSC meeting at the White House. The problem, of course, was that there were over four hundred people who worked in the White House. Narrowing them down to the few who might present a threat had been a challenge. Four had evaded their background check prior to the hostage taking at the NSC meeting. Four Trinity assassins had been embedded in the White House staff.

Those four were no longer a threat. But how

many more were slipping past them? The background checks didn't tell them much. They had to dive deeper into their private records, bank accounts, emails and phone records. The task was monumental given the number of White House staff.

The cell phone beside him buzzed with a text message. He glanced down at the screen. *Unknown Caller.*

His pulse beat faster as he unlocked the screen and stared down at the message.

Thank you.

Are you okay?

Yes.

Need a place to stay?

No.

If you do, I have room. So does Charlie.

Thanks.

Let me help more.

You are. Dig into Carpenter.

Will do. Be careful out there. I'm here whenever you need me.

Good to know.

Got a burner phone. Need to stop using this number in case it's being monitored. Call me for the number.

Cole waited, hoping she'd call. For several minutes, he didn't hear anything, text or voice. Then his personal cell phone chirped.

Unknown Caller.

"It's me," he answered.

"Number?" a female voice said.

He gave her the number and waited for more.

The call ended.

Disappointment piled onto frustration made Cole clench his fist. How could he do the job of protecting CJ if she wouldn't let him get close?

His burner phone vibrated. His pulse leaped and he lifted it to his ear. "It's me."

"It's me," she echoed.

Cole smiled. CJ's husky voice flowed over him like warm chocolate, oozing into every one of his pores.

"Better," he said. "Now, tell me…did you find a place to stay?"

"For now."

"Did you have any trouble getting away from the Trinity guy after you?"

"No."

She wasn't very forthcoming with information. Cole sighed. "What are my chances of actually seeing you so that I can protect you?"

She laughed, the sound like music in his ears. She almost sounded like a different person. "Slim to none. I don't need protection."

"Would you have made it out of the library without my help?"

"Yes."

"Did my assistance help you make it out without an altercation?"

She hesitated. "Yes. Thank you for the heads-up."

"It can't be easy searching the web on public computers. Charlie has a room full of computers in a secure location."

"Thanks, but I'll manage."

He felt her pulling away. "CJ?"

She didn't answer, but the line didn't go dead. Cole continued. "I really want to help you."

"Find the Director."

"We're working on it," he said, wanting to reach through the airwaves and grab her hand.

"I'll be in touch."

And the call ended.

Cole sighed. At least he'd heard from her and

gotten her onto a more secure line. He wanted her to be more tangible, to see her, touch her and know she was close so that he could protect her. At the same time, the woman was still alive after living a year outside of Trinity. She knew what she was doing and having someone else hanging around might slow her down.

Patience was never something Cole had in abundant supply.

He lifted his personal cell phone, not the burner phone he'd used with CJ, and dialed Charlie Halverson's estate.

Declan O'Neill answered. "Hey, Cole. Got anything new?"

"Heard from CJ."

"Good to know," Declan said. "Was wondering when she'd make contact."

"Dig into the Homeland Security Advisor, Chris Carpenter, since he'd texted Terrence Tully prior to the NSC incident."

"I'll get Jonah on it." Declan paused. "Did she say anything else?"

"No." Cole explained what had gone down with messages on the dark web and Trinity finding her at the library in Arlington.

"Does she need a place to stay? Charlie would happily put her up for as long as necessary."

Cole shook his head, though Declan couldn't see it. "She said she has a place for now. I gotta tell you, this assignment is killing me. How do I protect a woman I can't see?"

Declan chuckled. "It's like she's a ghost. Most likely she's gun-shy."

Cole snorted. "I know I would be if I had a target painted on my back. Trinity doesn't like to lose one of their own."

"To Trinity she's a loose end that needs to be tied up."

"With a bullet." Cole's jaw tightened.

"That's why you need to get closer to her and keep that from happening."

"Tell me about it." Declan was preaching to the choir. If only Cole could get close enough. Then he might be able to do his job.

In the meantime, all he could do was continue to sift through clues and data to find the Director.

Until CJ came out of the shadows, she was on her own.

Chapter Two

Contrary to what she'd told Cole, CJ didn't have a place to stay that first night after abandoning her apartment. She'd slept behind some bushes in a quiet neighborhood, leaving just before sunup to sneak into the twenty-four-hour gym she'd joined, paying for her annual membership in cash. After weight lifting and a run on the treadmill, she hit the shower and changed into clean clothes. She didn't think she'd be able to come back to the gym. Trinity had come too close the day before. If she was smart, she'd leave the DC area and start a new life in a different state. Hell, a different country wouldn't be far enough.

After a breakfast of a protein bar she had stashed in her backpack, she went in search of a new place to live. She'd done her own homework about the man assigned to protect her. Cole Mc-Castlain lived in a town house in Arlington.

Last night, CJ learned that a town house a few

doors down from the one Cole lived in was being sublet. The owners had just left on a world cruise and wouldn't be back for six months. She paid the deposit with money she'd earned designing web pages, gave her fake identification and quickly passed the background check. By noon, she had moved into the fully furnished home.

She didn't waste time settling in. While Cole and Declan's Defenders searched the web for information on Chris Carpenter, CJ would follow the man and learn what she could about his habits and who he talked to. She might be chasing shadows, but the text he'd sent to Tully prior to the NSC assault was all she had to go on. It could have meant nothing. The text could have been a legitimate effort to make sure all was in place, nothing more.

All other coordination for the meeting had been done via emails throughout the weeks prior to the get-together. A text would have been appropriate for a last-minute adjustment to the arrangements. Or it could have been information regarding the attack.

Though CJ had a laptop and could access the internet by tapping into Wi-Fi at internet cafés or libraries, she couldn't delve into the dark web anymore. Somehow, Trinity had found her and traced her IP address to the library. She could continue to hack into phone records and other sources of information, but they were getting too close.

Needing additional clothing and disguises, she shoved her hair up into a ball cap, dressed in a long gray sweater that hid her figure, and sunglasses. Disguised as best she could, CJ left the town house to visit a couple thrift shops. She found items that would help her to blend in and make her as invisible as possible. She even found a skirt suit that might come in handy if she wanted to get closer to some of the politicians on Capitol Hill. The total of her purchases barely made a dent in her cash. Afterward, she made a quick trip to the grocery store and stocked up on a few items she'd need to keep from having to eat fast foods. Once she'd unloaded the food and staples in the refrigerator and pantry, she put on a black wig, a different pair of glasses and a hooded sweatshirt and went out to scout the neighborhood thoroughly. Knowing where to go on short notice was always a good idea.

Stepping out on the sidewalk, she started toward Cole's place. On the bottom step of the next town house, a stooped old woman stood with one hand on a cane, the other on a leash. At the end of the leash was a white ball of fluff.

"Good afternoon," the woman called out with a smile. "You must be the one subletting the Anderson place."

Normally, CJ didn't stop to talk to anyone. But the woman and her dog didn't appear to pose a threat. "Yes, ma'am. I'm Rebecca." She didn't bother holding out her hand since the older woman's were both occupied.

The woman nodded. "Gladys Oliver."

CJ squatted beside the dog. "And who do we have here?" The little dog wiggled and jumped up on CJ, excited to meet someone new.

"Sweet Pea, named after one of my favorite flowers," Gladys said. "Down, girl." Her gentle tug on the dog's leash had little effect. "My granddaughter got me the dog, but she's still a puppy and needs a lot more exercise than these old bones can give her. I'm thinking I might have to give her back." The woman's brow furrowed. "She's such a sweet thing. I hate to give her up."

"I'm going for a walk now," CJ said. "I could take her with me, and she could burn off some energy, if you like."

The old woman's blue eyes brightened. "You would do that?"

"Certainly."

"I mean, it's not like you're really a stranger. I know where you live and all." Gladys handed over the leash. "She's really no trouble. Just needs to move a little faster than I do. If you're sure it's not a bother…"

"We'll do just fine together." CJ smiled at

Gladys. "We'll be back in twenty or thirty minutes."

"I'll be inside. Just knock when you're back. I'll come to the door." Gladys leaned down to pat the little dog on the head. "You be a good girl for Rebecca," she said and scratched Sweet Pea behind the ears.

Her disguise complete with a dog in tow, CJ walked along the sidewalk, letting Sweet Pea take her time sniffing every tree, mailbox, bush and blade of grass along the way. The dog's interest in her surroundings gave CJ plenty of time to study the homes, the street and places Trinity agents could be hiding, or where she could hide if she needed to.

Soon, she passed the town house where Cole lived. It looked much like the rest of the homes on the street. Two-story, narrow front, a four-foot-wide gap between it and the townhomes on either side, which she walked through to learn more. A five-foot-tall wooden fence surrounded a postage-stamp size backyard. Nothing CJ couldn't scale, if she had to. Without actually climbing the fence, she couldn't see what the back of the house had to offer in the way of doors, windows or trees. It was comforting to know he was only a few doors down from where she was staying.

She moved on, back to the front, studying the other houses and alleys all the way to the end of the long street where it turned onto a busy road. CJ turned left and kept walking, sticking to the sidewalk. A block away, there was a small strip mall with a hamburger place on one end and a pizza joint on the other. In between was a liquor store, a nail salon and an insurance agent.

Across the busy thoroughfare was a tattoo parlor, a pawnshop and a Chinese restaurant.

For the first few blocks, Sweet Pea led the way, tugging at the leash, eager to keep going. When she started to slow and hang back with CJ, it was time to turn around and get her home to her owner.

CJ performed an about-face and started back. When she turned the corner onto the street where she lived, her gaze went to Cole's place. She wondered if he was home. How easy would it be to stop in and say hello, like a regular person?

Still a few houses away, she heard the sound of running footsteps coming from behind.

CJ spun to face a man jogging toward her, wearing only shorts and running shoes. His body was poetry in motion, his muscles tight and well-defined. Every inch of exposed skin glistened with sweat.

Cole McCastlain. The man who wanted to be her protector.

She recognized him from the one time she'd been to Charlie Halverson's estate, immediately following the rescue of Anne Bellamy and the vice president of the United States. At that time, CJ hadn't been wearing a wig. She'd been without any disguise, her auburn hair hanging down around her shoulders.

Using the back of his arm, he wiped the sweat from his eyes and kept running toward her.

A tug on the leash reminded CJ of Sweet Pea. The dog had crossed the sidewalk to the opposite side, her leash creating a line in front of Cole. CJ crossed to the same side of the sidewalk to keep Cole from tripping over the leash.

He ran past her, the muscles in his legs flexing and tightening with each long stride.

A rush of relief washed over her, at the same time as a flush of heat.

The man had tone and definition in each muscle of his body, from his shoulders, down his chest, to his abs, thighs and calves. She bet she could bounce a quarter off his backside.

As he passed, he shot a sideways glance her way. For a brief moment, his eyes narrowed. He didn't slow, or stop, but kept moving. When he reached his town house, he ran up the steps and disappeared inside.

CJ inhaled a deep breath, amazed at how much she needed it. Had she forgotten how to breathe in the presence of the former marine? She told herself she wasn't ready to do anything that would

connect Cole to her. If Trinity was watching Declan's Defenders, and CJ was hanging out with
them, they'd find her and eliminate her before she
had a chance to expose the Director. She couldn't
let that happen. There were a lot of lost children,
teens and young adults being held captive and in-
doctrinated into the Trinity family of assassins.
They didn't deserve the life of violence for which
they were being groomed. The Director ruled the
organization with an iron fist. If they found and
destroyed the Director, Trinity would fold.

At least, that was the theory.

As she passed Cole's townhome, CJ kept her
face averted, focusing on the sidewalk in front of
her as if she were only out to walk her dog. In her
peripheral vision, she watched the windows for
movement. Was that him, standing in the corner
of the front picture window?

Her heart pounding, CJ kept moving, walking
past Gladys's house and her own for another block
before she returned.

The old woman met her at the door. "I thought I
saw you go by with Sweet Pea. I guess she needed
a little more of a walk." The woman leaned over,
her back hunched as she reached down to pet her
tired dog. "Thank you for taking Miss Sweet Pea
for a walk. I bet she sleeps all afternoon, now."
Gladys looked up. "Can I pay you for your trouble?"

CJ could always use the money, but she couldn't take it from the kind old woman. "No, ma'am. It was my pleasure. Sweet Pea must give you a great deal of comfort and companionship."

"She does. Since my children all grew up and moved away, and my husband passed, I've been lonely. Sweet Pea is my surrogate baby. I love her so much." The woman's eyes welled with unshed tears. "I'm sure you don't want to hear me blubbering about loneliness. But if you ever need a companion to walk with, Sweet Pea and I would be happy if you take her."

"Thank you, Ms. Gladys." On impulse, CJ leaned down and kissed the woman's cheeks. She reminded her of a grandmother she might once have known, who'd died before her parents' auto accident. Her heart swelled with emotions she hadn't felt in a very long time.

"Thank you again," she said and turned toward her town house.

"If you ever want to share a cup of tea or coffee, stop by anytime," Gladys called out. "I'd be happy to make some."

"I'll keep that in mind," CJ responded, knowing she couldn't do that. If Trinity was watching now, her short interaction with the old woman and her dog would place them in danger. Trinity wasn't above using others to lure their defectors out into the open. And they weren't above killing innocent people to get what they wanted.

And they wanted CJ dead.

WHEN COLE ENTERED his town house, he stopped long enough to catch his breath and then turned to the window. He could swear he knew the woman he'd jogged past, but he couldn't put his finger on who it was or where he'd known her.

The black hair wasn't ringing any bells. And the dog? He was certain he'd seen it with someone else. Didn't it belong to the old woman who lived several doors down from his place?

Maybe that was it. The woman was a daughter, granddaughter, niece or something to the old woman. Perhaps that was where he'd seen her before.

He waited at the window for her to pass with the dog. When they did, he looked hard, still unsure of where he'd seen her before. But he knew he had. The way she walked, the sway of her sexy hips, the tilt of her nose and the long, thick eyelashes should have been dead giveaways.

His phone rang in the armband he used when running. Cole tapped the earbud in his ear. "Yeah."

"You coming in to do some heavy-duty computing?" Declan O'Neill's voice sounded in his ear.

"I am. Just showering. I can be there in thirty to forty-five minutes."

"See ya then," Declan said.

When Cole glanced back out the window, the woman had disappeared, dog and all.

Cole showered, changed into jeans and a T-shirt and headed out to the Halverson estate, driving the Hummer he'd purchased prior to exiting the Marine Corps. Thankfully, Charlie Halverson had hired him before he'd had to sell it for money to live on until he'd gotten a decent-paying job.

Once he passed through the gates, he drove up the winding drive to the sprawling mansion.

Roger Arnold, Charlie's butler, met him at the door and let him in. "They're waiting for you in the war room," he said.

Cole went straight for the study and the trap-door that led into the basement of the mansion. All of Declan's Defenders were there.

Declan stood at a large whiteboard with photographs taped to the surface. Jonah Spradlin sat at a desk against the wall, an array of computer monitors displayed in front of him.

Mack Balkman sat in a chair near Declan. He ran a hand through his black hair, his blue eyes studying the whiteboard. Beside him sat the former Russian operative, Riley Lansing. Gus Walsh stood on the opposite side of the table, the woman he'd helped rescue standing at his side.

Jasmine Newman, aka Jane Doe, was as much a key to their operation as CJ Grainger. Jasmine had been a Trinity agent before John Halverson recruited her to help him fight the organization. Combat trained and fluent in Arabic and Russian, she was a formidable opponent and a worthy ally. They'd "killed" her off and given her a new name and identity to keep her off Trinity's hit list. So far, she'd managed to remain out of sight, but she would always be looking over her shoulder as long as Trinity remained a threat.

Jack Snow, the team slack man, sat beside Anne Bellamy, the mid-level staffer who'd been recruited by John Halverson to spy on politicians and staffers in the West Wing. She still had the bruises from her kidnapping ordeal by the Trinity sleeper agents a week before.

Frank "Mustang" Ford stood with his girl, Emily Chastain, the college professor. He turned as Cole entered the room. The brown-haired, brown-eyed former point man was as used to action as Cole. He paced the room like a caged cat. "Nice of you to join us."

Cole shook his head. "I'd have been here sooner, if I'd known you wanted me here." They were all tense. After the attack on the National Security Council meeting, they knew they had to bear down and come up with some real leads. Trinity had far too much power and had infiltrated too many places. Picking the agents off, one by one, would take too long and never be effective as the organization continued to "recruit" new agents. They had to find the lead man and take him down.

"Based on your woman's intel," Declan said, "Jonah's made some headway that might be useful." He turned to Charlie's computer guru.

Cole wanted to correct Declan. CJ wasn't his woman. He barely knew her and had seen her only once in the very room where he stood now. An image of a black-haired woman walking a little white dog rose in his mind.

Jonah pointed to one of the monitors. "Chris Carpenter is in debt up to his eyeballs. He's maxed out every credit card he owns—and he has quite a few—and he's struggling to make the minimum payments on all those. He's in a house that far exceeds his pay scale and he's gone through everything his father left him in a trust fund."

"The man is barely able to keep his head above water," Declan concluded. "It's a wonder he got a security clearance."

Cole shrugged. "CJ thought he might have a connection to Trinity since his was one of the last texts Tully received on his cell phone prior to the attack on the NSC conference room. How does his financial woes make him a likely suspect?"

"A man that deep in debt can usually be bought," a female voice said from behind Cole.

He turned to face Charlie descending the stairs,

carrying a tray loaded with glasses and a pitcher of lemonade.

The butler followed with another tray of sandwiches Cole suspected were prepared by Charlie's chef, Carl.

Cole took the tray from her and set it on the conference table.

Charlie took over hostess duties, pouring lemonade into clear, crystal glasses. "It's not whiskey, but then I thought you might want to have clear heads for this discussion."

She handed out glasses to everyone who wanted one and then nodded toward the picture of Carpenter that had been taped to the whiteboard. "If Carpenter is in debt that deep, an offer to bail him out might convince him to do favors for anyone who is willing to pay for them."

"I've worked with Chris Carpenter for the past two years." Anne Bellamy shook her head. "It's hard to believe he would work for Trinity."

"Desperation changes a man," Charlie said. "If he's in over his head and drowning, he'll take any life raft thrown his way to get out."

"Just because he's in debt, doesn't make him a traitor," Cole said. "We need solid proof. Got anything else?"

Jonah's lips twisted and his gaze narrowed. "He's made several payments to a marriage counseling center."

Cole sighed. "Again, a marriage on the rocks isn't much to go on."

"We need more," Declan agreed. "Do you have access to CJ?"

"We're communicating by burner phones," Cole said, and held up the phone he'd purchased for just that purpose.

"Get her on the line," Declan commanded.

"I can't guarantee she'll answer," Cole said. "She's very skittish."

"That's the only way she can stay alive if Trinity is actively pursuing her," Jasmine said. "It's a miracle she's still alive after escaping over a year ago. And to be in an area known to be prime Trinity territory..." The former assassin shook her head.

Cole hit the redial button on his phone.

After the fourth ring, CJ answered. "What did you find?" she asked without preamble.

"I'm with the team. Can I put you on speaker?"

"Yes."

Cole hit the speaker button. "We learned more about Carpenter, but not enough to accuse him of conspiring with Trinity." He filled her in on the Homeland Security Advisor's financial troubles and the fact that he was seeing a marriage counselor.

"I doubt he's meeting with any Trinity contacts inside the West Wing. I'll follow him," CJ said.

"That puts you at too much risk of being discovered," Cole insisted. "I'll follow him and let you know what I find."

"I've seen him go into a bar close to the metro station after work," Anne Bellamy interjected. She gave them the name of the bar and the street where it was located.

"Anne and I will keep an eye on him in the West Wing during the day," Jack offered. He was still posing as Anne's office assistant.

Anne nodded. "We can follow him at lunch and see if he talks with anyone."

"Good," Cole said. "But he knows you two and wouldn't want you to know who he's meeting with. I'll go to the bar tomorrow night ahead of him. He doesn't know me and won't think anything of me sitting there sipping on a beer."

"I can let you know what time he leaves," Jack added. "And follow him in case he doesn't head for the bar."

"Deal," Cole said. "CJ, we'll keep you informed."

"Understood," she concurred and ended the call.

"Not a woman of many words," Gus noted.

Cole snorted. "No, she's not."

"You've heard the phrase 'loose lips sink ships'?" Jasmine asked.

"Yeah, but she's like a ghost. If she hadn't shown

up after the NSC attack, here in this room, in front of all of us, I'd still wonder if she exists."

"She wants to bring down Trinity," Anne Bellamy said.

Cole silently agreed. They all wanted to bring down Trinity. He understood CJ's reluctance to trust anyone but herself with her life, but she didn't know the benefits of working with a good team, one that had her back and was pushing toward the same goal.

"And she can't do it if she's dead," Charlie reminded them, her mouth set in a grim line. "As we all know. John wanted to bring down Trinity, but look where that got him."

John Halverson had been murdered. The person who'd done it had never been caught.

Cole had no intention of being Trinity's next target. And something in him stilled at the thought of CJ meeting John Halverson's fate.

Not on his watch.

Chapter Three

CJ spent the next day logged on to her laptop at a coffee shop with free Wi-Fi. It was an unsecured network, but sometimes she found being one needle in a haystack of browser users helped mask her more than logging on to unique systems with huge firewalls. Trinity had a way around firewalls. She'd searched for the first half of the day, tapping into computers, trying to find the IP address for Chris Carpenter's home computer and digging into the man's bank and phone records.

She didn't find any large sums of money deposited to Carpenter's account. If he was involved with Trinity, he might have a secret account set up in a foreign location like the Cayman Islands. She'd need access to whatever computer he used to find whatever information he might have stored regarding secret accounts and passwords. In the meantime, she wanted to follow Carpenter to find out for herself if he was meeting with anyone who had any connection to Trinity.

After a lunch of a peanut butter and jelly sandwich, she donned the black wig, knocked on Gladys's door and took Sweet Pea for a walk, going the opposite direction from Cole's town house. Somehow, she managed to stroll around several blocks, making a complete circle that landed her in front of Cole's place, though. He didn't jog by this time, and she didn't see him peering through his window, looking for her.

A stab of disappointment struck her. She couldn't understand why. She'd bet her life on remaining alone. Why would seeing a stranger occasionally mean anything to her?

Because, after a year of being alone, she knew there were people out there who had her best interests at heart. She wasn't truly alone anymore. And it felt good.

That thought warmed her cold soul. For too long, she'd had to squelch all emotions. Her training with Trinity had emphasized that point. Any recruit who cried was punished severely. After one or two beatings, she'd learned to hold back her emotions, to swallow the tears and get tough. By doing so, she lessened or erased the pain.

When she'd been tasked with killing the pregnant woman, it had been the first crack in the wall she'd built around her heart. Having the backing of Declan's Defenders was chinking away at more of the mortar that held her emotions at bay. Talking via voice or text with Cole reminded her of the vulnerability of emotions. It scared her to open up to anyone, to leave herself exposed to the kindness of others.

Hell, even the happiness Sweet Pea displayed when she'd come to take her for a walk had pinched CJ's heart. She needed to be alone, to remain aloof, to fight her own battles.

But Trinity was bigger than one person could deal with. She'd had to get help. She'd had to trust others to get the job done.

After she left Sweet Pea with Gladys, she went back to her sublet town house, showered and changed into a little black dress she'd picked up at the secondhand store, black heels and the long blond wig. Taking a circuitous route to the nearest station, she rode the metro into DC and got off near the pub Carpenter frequented.

She arrived well before five o'clock, found a stool at the far end of the bar and ordered vodka and cranberry juice, figuring it was girlie enough for a blonde woman wearing a sexy black dress. CJ preferred whiskey or beer, but the drink was cool and refreshing. Now all she had to do was wait for Carpenter to arrive.

If he arrived.

The first thirty minutes passed with a couple

tourists wandering in and ordering beer. They left after they'd finished their beers to find someplace to eat.

The bartender asked a couple of times if he could get her another drink, which CJ politely declined.

A glance at the time on her cell phone indicated it was well past five thirty and creeping up on six. CJ had begun to think Carpenter wouldn't make his usual stop and her time there would have been a waste.

Then the door opened and a man in a dark gray suit entered and found a table in a shadowy corner.

From the pictures CJ had found online, the man was Chris Carpenter.

She studied him out of the corner of her eye, taking in the nice suit and tie, the highly polished shoes and the fact that he was staring at the entrance as if he was worried or expecting someone.

CJ kept her head down, watched and waited.

A couple minutes later, another man walked through the door and took a seat at the bar. He wore an Atlanta Braves baseball cap, jeans and a Led Zeppelin revival T-shirt. After ordering a drink, he removed the cap and ran his fingers through his hair, making it stand on end. He ordered the whiskey CJ wished she was drinking.

When he turned his profile toward her, she sucked in a sharp breath.

Cole.

She couldn't forget the close-cropped, dark brown hair, square jaw and his nose that wasn't quite straight but had a bump in it like it had been broken at some point in his life.

Another man walked through the door and sat on one of the stools in between CJ and Cole. He ordered a draft beer. When the tall mug came, he lifted it, turned in his seat and looked around the bar.

Was this a man who'd come to talk to a traitor?

CJ stared at the mirror behind the bar, watching the man's every move. He turned to her, got off his stool and moved to the one next to her.

He hitched his leg up on the stool and set his mug on the bar. Then he leaned toward her. "Hey, beautiful, you come here often?"

She shook her head, not wanting to start a conversation with him.

"Can I buy you a drink?"

Again, she shook her head and lifted the half-empty glass of the drink she'd been nursing for the past hour and a half. The ice had melted and the liquid had grown lukewarm. CJ didn't care. She didn't want another drink as much as she wanted to find the leader of Trinity and put an end to the terror.

"Not much of a talker, are you?" the man said and leaned closer. "That's okay, talk is overrated.

What say you and I go get some supper, then find a place with some music?"

The idiot couldn't take ignoring him as an answer. Apparently, he had to have things spelled out for him.

CJ drew in a deep breath and spoke softly but with a steely edge. "I'm not interested."

"If you want to wait until you finish your drink, I'm flexible," the man said.

She didn't look at the man, just set her drink on the bar and started talking.

"Sir, I'm not interested in drinking, eating or sleeping with you, now or in the future. You might as well move on."

The man's lips pressed into a thin line. "I'm being really nice. Asking all polite, and everything."

CJ slipped to the edge of her bar stool, ready to take the man down if he so much as touched her. Meanwhile, a brunette, wearing a slim-line black skirt with a white button-down blouse, entered the bar, pushed a long strand of her chocolate-brown hair out of her face and looked around, as if trying to get her eyes to adjust to dim lighting. After a few minutes, she scanned the interior. She must have found who she was looking for because she didn't stand around long. Hiking her cross-body purse up onto her shoulder, she walked past Cole, CJ and the man bugging the fire out of her and slipped into the booth beside Chris Carpenter's. She sat with her back to Chris.

"You sure look hungry," the guy beside CJ was saying. "What would it hurt for you to come share a meal with me?" Obnoxious Man couldn't get the hint that his attention was unwanted.

"Darla, honey." The familiar male voice cut into Obnoxious Man's continued pressuring. "I'm sorry I was late." Cole slipped an arm over her shoulder and bent to brush a kiss across her lips.

CJ was so surprised, she forgot to breathe. When Cole set her at arm's length, he turned to the man beside her. "Do I have you to thank for keeping my fiancée company while she waited for me to get off work?"

The man's brow furrowed. "Don't know what you're talking about. Didn't know the lady was spoken for." And obviously hadn't seen Cole sitting at the bar a few stools away.

"No worries," Cole said. "My baby knows how to take care of herself." He winked and looked down at CJ. "Ready to go? We have a few stops on the way home."

She smiled, though she wanted to frown. What was his game? Then she shot a glance at the booth where Chris Carpenter had been sitting. He was gone. And so was the female who'd sat in the booth beside his.

CJ hopped up from her stool, slipped her arm

through Cole's and started for the door, muttering beneath her breath, "How did you know it was me?"

"Wasn't positive at first, but once the light shone on your green eyes, I knew." He grinned as he held the door for her to leave the bar and step out onto the sidewalk.

"We've met only once before. How did you remember I had green eyes?"

He shook his head. "They reminded me of the color of the live oak leaves on the trees back home in Texas, but that would be a lie. They are actually the color of the paint job on my Hummer, a kind of gray-olive color."

CJ glanced left then right, not seeing their quarry immediately. "I'm not quite sure if that's an insult or a compliment, and I really don't care. Do you see him?"

Cole had been looking. "There. Looks like he's headed for the metro."

"Let's catch him before he gets away."

Cole had replaced his ball cap on his head. Taking her hand, he walked at a quick pace.

Though several inches shorter than Cole, CJ kept up with him and they made it to the station at the same time Chris Carpenter climbed aboard the train with the same woman who'd been sitting in the booth beside his.

COLE SPOTTED CHRIS and a woman stepping onto the train. He hurried CJ along and entered a different car before the doors shut and the train slid out of the station.

"Any idea who the woman is?" CJ asked beside him. Like him, she was staring through the windows separating their car from the next one.

Carpenter and the woman sat side by side, facing them. Cole didn't recognize her, but based on her business suit, she probably worked somewhere on Capitol Hill or in one of the business offices nearby.

What her relationship with Carpenter was, Cole could only guess. They didn't hold hands, touch or even talk to each other. But they sat together.

Cole glanced at the train map on the inside of the car. They were headed toward Arlington, Virginia. He noted that the train had several stops to make as it moved through the city toward the countryside.

Carpenter and his lady friend weren't on for long. At the second stop, they got off.

Cole and CJ stood at the exit to their car until Carpenter passed. Once they were well past them, Cole and CJ left the train and followed Carpenter and the woman to a hotel.

"I guess that explains why he's seeing a marriage counselor," CJ said.

"I'd bet my last dollar that woman he was with wasn't his wife," Cole said.

"Is it worth hanging out to find out for sure?"

"You can if you want," Cole said. "But I'm thinking it might be a good idea to plot our next move. With Carpenter being a creature of habit and going to the bar every day after work and getting a little frisky afterward, we might use that time to get into his home computer."

"You think, like I do, that he'd keep any information of value on his computer at home?"

Cole shrugged. "It would be safer at home than in the West Wing. We just need to ascertain Mrs. Carpenter's schedule and work around it."

"Tomorrow night, maybe?" CJ confirmed. "That would give us time to figure out the best plan."

"Tomorrow, as long as Mrs. C is also out of the house."

CJ held out her hand to Cole. "We're on for tomorrow night."

"Partners?" Cole took her hand in his, an electric awareness zipping up his arm and spreading throughout his body.

Her eyes narrowed. "I like to work alone. But I guess it would be better to have someone looking out for me."

"Then it's a date." Cole grinned.

"If breaking and entering someone's home is

what you consider a date," CJ said, "then I guess it is."

Cole grinned all the way back to the metro. When they got on the same train heading farther into Arlington, he leaned close to her and asked. "So that was you yesterday with the black hair, walking the white dog, wasn't it?"

CJ's chin lifted. "I don't know what you're talking about."

Cole's grin broadened. "Right." He'd bet his favorite semiautomatic rifle that he was right.

Working with CJ would be a challenge. The first part of which would be getting her to trust him enough to stick around.

For a late-evening ride, the train was still crowded with people trying to get home from the city.

Aware of the fact Trinity wanted CJ dead, Cole kept a vigilant watch on the passengers, considering each and every one of them a potential Trinity agent.

A couple passengers, in particular, captured his attention. Every time he looked over at them, they were staring at CJ. Granted, in the little black dress and the blond wig, she was a knockout. But there was something else. A furtiveness about them. When they thought someone was watching them, they looked away quickly.

One was a young man wearing jeans and a brown leather jacket, his hands in the pockets.

Cole moved to place his body between the young man and CJ in case one of those pockets contained a handgun.

The other potential Trinity operative was a woman with long black hair and dark eyes. Tall, slim and athletic, she looked like she could take down a linebacker with a few well-placed side kicks to the knees.

"Is it getting warm in here to you?" CJ murmured in a low tone.

He understood what she was talking about. "Could be."

The train rolled into a station three stops from the one closest to his town house. A few people got off, but not the two Cole had his eye on.

A second before the train doors were due to close, CJ slipped out.

Cole didn't have time to react before the doors closed and the train jerked into motion.

The two people he'd been watching turned toward the platform as the train left the station.

Already, CJ had disappeared from sight.

Cole worried for her safety. Trinity agents didn't give up easily. But then CJ had survived for a year on her own. She knew how to escape and evade.

Having been a part of a combat team, Cole

knew a little about stealth and camouflage. CJ brought it to an entirely different level. He hoped that by teaming with her, he didn't put her at more of a risk than she already was. If Trinity thought he could be an asset they could hold over her to force her out into the open, they wouldn't hesitate to use him. With that in mind, he pulled the same stunt as CJ at the next stop. He waited until the last moment.

As the doors started to slide closed, he stepped out onto the platform. The doors closed with the two people he'd been watching staring at him through narrowed eyes.

Cole didn't wait around for anyone else to catch up with him. He took off on foot and jogged the rest of the way to his town house, taking a twisting, turning route, checking behind him as he went to make certain no one was following. Not that it would make a big difference. If someone wanted to find him, they could. His whereabouts weren't a secret like CJ's.

When he arrived at his place, he entered, locked the door and checked all the other locks to ensure they were secure.

Once he was certain he was alone and fairly safe, he texted CJ. Make it back?

No response.

Cole waited for the next hour, giving her time to return. When she still didn't respond, he called

Declan and reported on the night. Declan promised to swing into action if needed but urged him to hang tight a while longer in case CJ came home.

He stayed awake for a long time, wondering if she was still alive and what he could have done differently to keep her from getting away without him.

He knew he couldn't have acted any faster. She had the advantage. CJ knew what she was going to do next. No one else did. Hopefully, that paid off for her and kept her alive until they could bring Trinity down.

Chapter Four

When CJ got off the train three stops short of the one leading to her sublet, she knew she had a tail. She'd hoped that by getting off at the last minute, she'd shaken any follower. Unfortunately, he'd been watching closely and hadn't been in the same car with her, so she'd not seen him until it was too late.

As soon as she stepped off the train, he dived out of the other car.

CJ quickly left the station, moving among other passengers in a hurry to the parking lot where commuters left their vehicles to catch the train into DC. When she made it to a line of cars, she ducked low, rolled under an SUV and rummaged in the satchel she'd carried in place of her usual backpack. Quickly taking off the wig, she stuffed it into the bag, pulled out a baseball cap and wound her hair up into it.

The dress was a little more difficult. Lying

beneath a vehicle, she couldn't get out of it. Instead, she removed her heels, pulled out a pair of sweats, slipped them up her legs and over the short dress. CJ struggled into a hooded sweat jacket and zipped it. She slipped on her running shoes, shoved her heels into the bag and tucked the bag under her jacket.

When she was ready, she remained where she was, timing her move for when the next train was due to arrive. She looked beneath the chassis of the vehicles, searching for the feet of her pursuer. When the time came, and she didn't see any movement, she rolled out from under the SUV and straightened slowly.

Figuring her tail would be looking for her to move away from the train station, she hunkered over like a fat man in a tracksuit and lumbered toward the metro stop, arriving at the same time as a train pulled in.

Men and women in business clothing got off the train, their faces tired, their clothing creased from hours of sitting behind desks. As soon as the car emptied of the passengers for that stop, CJ boarded and found a seat near the door, dropped into it and pulled her ball cap low over her face. The man she'd seen get off the train when she had was nowhere in sight. She'd checked as she'd gotten on, looking in the other cars on either side of the one she'd stepped into.

Only a few people remained on the train headed out of DC into the neighboring municipalities, all looking like they'd had a long day and were ready to be home.

CJ stayed on a stop past the one closest to her rented town house. She didn't trust that she was still alone, though she'd lost her last follower. Always vigilant, she would walk the extra blocks to save herself from being caught.

By the time she arrived at her sublet, she was exhausted and took only a few minutes to unpack her satchel and repack her backpack with clothing she might need for quick changes the next day.

She dug out the burner phone from the satchel and glanced down at a text from Cole: Make it back?

Her heart warmed. He wanted to make sure she'd returned to her place safely. Whether it was because she was his assignment didn't matter. Someone cared enough to ask. Her fingers hovered over the letters that could spell out a response, but she held back. The more she relied on him, the more vulnerable she became, the more at risk he became. Shoving the phone into a pocket on the side of the backpack, she finished packing it for the next day.

CJ took the pack with her into the bathroom, brushed out the three wigs she kept on hand and packed them into one of the large pockets. When she was done, she stripped out of the jacket, sweats and dress, and climbed into the shower.

For the next twenty minutes, she let the water wash over her, the spray pounding into her shoulders, easing the tension. When her skin started to shrivel, she shut off the water, grabbed a towel and dried her body. As she stepped out of the shower, she heard something that sounded a lot like breaking glass.

Immediately alert, she slipped into a T-shirt and the sweatpants she'd removed minutes before and jammed her feet into the running shoes. Quietly opening the door to the bathroom, she eased out with her backpack, hurried to the bedroom door, closed and locked it quietly.

Downstairs, she could hear the crunch of someone walking over the broken glass in heavy shoes or boots. CJ opened the French doors off the master bedroom and stepped out onto the balcony overlooking the minuscule backyard, carefully closing the door behind her.

Knowing she had only moments to spare, she slipped the backpack over her shoulders, grabbed the balcony railing and eased her legs over the edge. She lowered her body, holding on to the railing until she was as close to the ground as she could get, and let go.

When her feet hit the ground, she bent her knees and rolled onto her side to absorb the impact. A crash above indicated her intruder had smashed through the master bedroom door.

Her heart thudding against her ribs, CJ sprang to her feet and ran as fast as she could, diving into the shadows of the town house next door. She kept moving, clinging to the shadows until she came to the town house Cole lived in.

For a moment, she considered running past and disappearing into the night. Leaving Cole out of her life was the right thing to do. He could easily become collateral damage in Trinity's quest to bring her down.

But CJ was tired.

Tired of running. Tired of fighting this battle. Tired of being alone. Knowing she would regret it later, she stopped and peered through a gap in the blinds. Cole sat in a chair, a beer in one hand, his burner phone in the other. Was he waiting for her response to his earlier question?

Before she could change her mind, she tapped on the window softly. If he didn't hear it, she would move on. She couldn't make a lot of noise and she didn't have time to stand around. Her intruder would soon figure out that she'd jumped off the balcony and would be hot on her trail.

CJ glanced around, her pulse thundering, her muscles tense, ready to move out swiftly if she needed to run.

When she looked back through the gap in the

blinds, she didn't see Cole sitting in the same spot. In fact, she didn't see him at all.

Then the back door to the town house opened and the barrel of a gun poked out, followed by Cole's head.

"Don't shoot," CJ whispered. "It's me, CJ."

"What the hell?" he said in a hushed tone.

CJ hurried toward him.

When she came within reach, he grabbed her arm and yanked her through the door, closing it softly behind him.

The first thing CJ did was move out of the site of the door frame and deeper into the house, turning off lights as she went.

Cole followed her, his gun still gripped in his hand. "What's going on?"

"What? I thought you wanted to be a little closer so that you could protect me," she said as she closed even the slightest gaps in the blinds. The only light illuminating the rooms came from the streetlamp in front of the town house shining around the edges of the curtains.

Cole's hand on her arm brought her to a stop. "Seriously, what happened? Why did you ditch me on the train?"

She shrugged. "We had a tail, so I got off." CJ glanced away, her lips thinning. "My tail got off at the same time."

"Damn it, CJ." Cole's fingers gripped her shoulders, forcing her to face him. "How can I help you, if you don't let me?"

Her chin rose and she stared straight into his eyes. "What could you do that I didn't?"

"What did you do?"

"I hid, changed disguises and waited for the next train. When I got on, he didn't." She breathed in a deep breath and let it out. "But he found where I lived and broke in."

Cole swore again. "That's it. You're staying with me." He held up a hand. "I don't want to hear any argument. You and I are going to be like Siamese twins, joined at the hips."

Her lips twitched, a smile forming. His words struck her as funny. If she wasn't in such a hurry to get away from whoever was following her, she might have laughed at the image his words invoked. "We can't stay here. If he found me once, he'll find me again."

"Give me a second to put on shoes." He moved her to the shadows of the hallway and pointed at her chest. "Stay."

"I'm not a dog."

His eyes narrowed. "On second thought…" Cole took her hand and led her into his bedroom. "I'm keeping an eye on you. You have a habit of slipping away."

"I won't this time," she promised.

"Yeah. And I'm supposed to believe that?" He shook his head and stripped out of his sweatpants.

CJ's eyes widened at the boxer briefs he wore beneath them. They fit his tight backside like a second skin. When Cole turned to face her as he shook out a pair of jeans, CJ's breath caught in her throat.

The thick bulge in front was evidence the man was built and that he was a little turned on at the moment.

He jammed his legs into the jeans and pulled them up and over the hard ridge.

CJ was almost sad he'd zipped himself into the tight denims.

He didn't bother to tuck in his T-shirt; instead, he pushed his arms into a leather jacket and shrugged it on over his shoulders. "Ready?"

She snorted. "Always. You're the one that needed to get dressed." CJ glanced around. "Got a ride?"

"In the garage."

"If we go out, he'll see us leaving."

"Then we go out with you tucked down low."

"If they know where to find me, they might also know you're involved with me in some way. That makes you as much of a target as I am." She shook her head. "I shouldn't have come."

"Too late. You did. I'm stuck with you, and we're getting out of here together." He winked. "Trust me. I'm smarter than you think."

CJ knew he'd been a competent marine, or he wouldn't have made it into the elite Marine Force Reconnaissance. But how would they get the vehicle out of the garage without attracting the attention of the man who'd broken into her town house?

The answer was…they wouldn't.

COLE INSTRUCTED CJ TO get down on the floorboard as he jumped into the driver's seat. His Hummer was facing out. He almost always backed into his garage so he could be ready to roll whenever duty called. As he jabbed the automatic door opener button on his visor, he started the engine.

Like a thief who'd just robbed a bank, Cole stomped on the accelerator and roared out of the garage onto the street, turning away from the town house CJ said she had occupied.

Just when he thought he'd made it out without encountering resistance, the back window of his Hummer exploded, spitting glass through the interior. Since the bullet hadn't gone all the way through the front windshield, Cole assumed it had lodged into the back of one of the seats.

He didn't wait around for a repeat performance. His foot pressed all the way to the floor, he raced down the street, putting as much distance as he could between them and the active shooter. Three blocks farther, he turned onto another road. If the shooter had a vehicle or a driver waiting nearby, they could catch up to them. The Hummer wasn't known for being a great getaway vehicle. Thus, distance before the shooter could mount up was key.

"CJ?"

"Yeah," she replied.

"You all right?" he asked.

She unfolded, sliding up into the passenger seat. "I'm okay." Looking over her shoulder at the shattered back window, she grimaced. "Which is more than I can say for your vehicle. I'm sorry. I shouldn't have come to you."

"Don't say that. The window can be replaced. If you had been hit…" Cole shook his head. "Well… dead is dead. There's no replacing someone."

CJ snorted. "There would be no need to replace me. I don't have a family who depends on me. Really, no one would care whether I lived or died."

Cole reached out and took her hand in his. "I'd care."

She gave him a weak smile. "Don't feel like you have to humor me."

"Don't worry. I won't feel obligated." His lips twisted. "Now, quit feeling sorry for yourself and keep your eyes peeled for anyone following us."

"Gotcha." CJ turned in her seat and peered through the shattered glass.

Racing through the residential streets of Arlington, he avoided the main arteries and aimed for one of the side roads that led to the Halverson estate. Whoever had guessed he and CJ had a connection would also know the connection Cole had to Charlie Halverson. After the kidnapping and subsequent rescue of the vice president of the United States, more people would know of the existence of Declan's Defenders. If not by the team's moniker, then by their personal names. If anyone was following Cole and CJ, they'd soon discover the meeting location at the Halverson estate.

In which case, he should get there as quickly as possible to avoid any Trinity agents who might try to beat him by using a more direct route.

He thought of calling ahead to let the team know he'd be coming in, possibly with a tail, but he put all his focus on the drive instead, mapping out the best route in his head. He'd phone when they were closer and knew more.

Finally on the country road leading to Charlie's estate, Cole increased his speed, determined to get inside the safety of the Halverson gates and wall.

At every curve, he slowed, expecting to find a vehicle blocking the road on the other side of the bend. Coming out of the last turn, he could almost taste the home stretch to the gate. That's when he saw something lying across the road. It appeared flat, like maybe a strip of construction material that had fallen off the back of a truck. It was hard to make it out in the dark. He didn't have enough time to slow down before he reached it.

He was going fifty miles per hour when, at the last minute, he saw what it was and slammed on the brakes. Too late. His tires hit the spike strip and exploded.

"Get down!" Cole cried out.

The steering wheel jerked in his hands. He held on as best he could but had little effect as each tire hit the spikes. His Hummer careened out of control and skidded on flat tires and bare metal rims on the pavement. When they ran out of pavement, the metal wheels dug into the shoulder and the vehicle flipped, rolling down into the ditch, landing, by some miracle, upright, airbags deploying and pushing them both back in their seats.

"Get out!" CJ yelled. "Get out and run!" She struggled with the airbag and her door. When she couldn't get it open, she used the gun in her hand and hit it with the grip, breaking through the window. With the barrel, she cleaned away the jagged pieces, grabbed her backpack, pulled herself through and dropped to the ground.

It took Cole several attempts before he finally managed to shove open his door. He reached into the glove box, grabbed his handgun and dropped out.

"Run!" CJ shouted, already halfway up the other side of the ditch, heading into the darker shadows of the woods.

Cole stumbled, then found his footing and raced after her.

He'd barely reached the tree line when he heard a blast. Less than a second later, he was thrown to the ground by the force of an explosion. Metal, glass and fragments of what had once been his Hummer filled the air around him.

His ears rang as he pushed to his knees and searched the gloom for CJ.

Over his shoulder, flames rose from the burning fuel that had spilled onto the road.

Movement captured his attention out of the corner of his vision.

Slinging her backpack over her shoulders, CJ staggered to her feet, her body visible in the light from the fire and silhouetted against the darkness of the trees.

Though his head spun, and his ears rang, he realized that if he could see CJ, others could, too. Could see both of them. Hunkering low, he ran toward CJ.

"Get down," he said as he got close. "Get down!" When she didn't drop fast enough, he hit her from behind, tackling her like a linebacker.

She crashed to the ground as the sound of gunfire echoed through the trees and splinters of bark rained down on them.

The rapid report of multiple rounds being popped off indicated the shooter had a semiautomatic rifle.

"Move, but stay low," Cole urged. On his hands and knees, he clung to the shadows, following CJ as she crawled through the underbrush, moving deeper into the woods.

Crouched as they were, they wouldn't stay ahead of their attackers for long. Though his eyes had adjusted to the darkness, it was difficult to know which way they were going. As long as they kept moving away from the light of the fire, they were headed in the right direction.

The gunfire ceased and silence stretched like a bad dream. Any movement made noise when they crossed over dried leaves and twigs. But it couldn't be helped. They didn't have armored vests and helmets to protect them from gunfire. And Cole didn't have his M4A1 rifle to fire back. He'd have to get close enough to use a pistol to kill his opponents. That was too risky.

When he thought they were out of range of the rifle, Cole pushed to his feet.

CJ rose, as well.

Grabbing her hand, he took off running, zigzagging through the trees.

Not ten seconds later, gunfire announced that their pursuers weren't far behind.

Finding a wall of brush, Cole pulled CJ in behind it. Together, they lay low to the ground and waited. Perhaps someone would notify the police of the fire by the road. Hopefully, they could hold out long enough for help to arrive.

If not, Cole would wait until their opponents passed in front of them. At that point, he'd have a chance of hitting his targets with the handgun he'd jammed into his waistband.

Footsteps crashed through the underbrush, heading toward them.

With the barrel of his Glock, Cole pushed aside the brush and peered through the opening.

Two men ran through the woods, carrying what appeared to be AR-15 rifles. The lead man aimed ahead and fired several rounds.

Cole and CJ ducked as low to the ground as they could get.

A siren wailed in the distance.

At first, the men running toward them didn't hear the emergency vehicle's alarm. They were almost to where Cole and CJ lay hidden when they stopped running and listened.

One swore. "Gotta get back to the vehicle."

"What about our target?" the other asked.

"Can't stay, or they'll find our van. Empty your clip. Maybe we'll get lucky." The lead guy turned and fired into the trees. His partner did the same.

Cole moved, covering CJ's body with his as the barrage continued for the next thirty seconds.

He lay still and waited, even after the gunfire ceased. Afraid to make a sound, he didn't dare move.

The shuffle of feet indicated the men were moving again, heading back the way they'd come.

As their footsteps faded, Cole moved off CJ's back and looked through the bushes.

Their pursuers were gone.

Cole remained hidden behind the greenery for another full minute before he spoke. "Clear."

CJ rose up to a kneeling position. "The fire's dying down."

The siren grew louder. Through the trees, they could see the flashing lights of a fire engine and the blue lights of a law-enforcement vehicle.

Cole stood and held out his hand.

CJ took it and let him draw her to her feet.

They walked back through the woods, hand in hand.

As they neared the scene of the explosion, CJ stopped in the shadows. "I'd rather not make my presence known."

Cole nodded. "Follow this road for a quarter of a mile to get past this circus. I'll call to have one of the guys come get us. But right now, I need to let the fire department and law-enforcement personnel know the driver of that burning vehicle is not dead." When CJ turned, Cole held on to her hand, forcing her to stop. "Promise me you'll be there when I shake loose of this mess."

She hesitated for a moment.

Cole squeezed her hand gently. "You've trusted me so far, why stop now?"

Her fingers tightened around his. "I'll be there."

Not sure he trusted her to keep her word, Cole pulled his gun out of his waistband and laid it in her hand that he'd been holding. "Take this. I don't want to have to declare it to the law."

She slipped it into one of her jacket pockets.

"CJ?" He cupped her cheek in his palm. "We're going to figure this out. I promise."

She looked up, the lights from the fire engine flashing in her eyes. "That's the plan."

He bent and brushed his lips across hers. "Not just a plan." He kissed her again. "A promise." He pulled her close, crushing her in his arms, his mouth coming down over hers.

Her body stiffened in his arms. But as he continued to kiss her, she relaxed, melting against him, her lips opening to him. Her hands crept up around his neck and she leaned into him.

For a long moment, the world faded away around them and Cole caressed the back of CJ's neck and slid his tongue along hers in a kiss he didn't want to end.

When he raised his head, he let go and stood back.

CJ touched a hand to her lips. "Why did you do that?"

"I don't know." He reached out and brushed his

knuckles across her cheek. "But if you don't go now, I'll do it again."

She caught his hand in hers and pressed her lips into his palm. Then she turned and ran. CJ moved like a cat, slipping through the darkness, her supple body all grace in motion.

Once he was certain she was far enough out of range, Cole pulled his phone out of his pocket and called Declan.

"Cole. Tell me you aren't on the highway headed to Charlie's?"

"Sorry, but I was."

"We heard an explosion and came out to see what was going on. Was that you?" Declan asked.

"Afraid so. I was on my way to Charlie's when all hell broke loose." Cole explained what happened from CJ showing up at his door to the men blowing up his Hummer. "We're going to need a ride to Charlie's after I check in with the first responders. I'm supposed to meet CJ a quarter mile from the scene. She might have passed you in the darkness. She probably won't come out until I show up."

"Got it. We'll turn around and wait for you to come out. I'll let Charlie know. She might have some connections to get you out of there sooner rather than later."

"Thanks." Cole ended the call and emerged onto the highway amid the emergency vehicles.

At the center of the crew working the fire, Cole found the sheriff and firefighter in charge. While he gave them a rundown on what had happened, he was careful not to mention anything that had occurred prior to his being on the road where the incident had occurred. He pretended he didn't have any idea why someone would want to attack him.

Once the sheriff and the fire chief finished with him, he gave them his phone number and promised to be available to answer any further questions that arose.

"Need a ride?" the sheriff's deputy asked.

"No, thank you," Cole responded. "Already called a friend." He left the emergency crews doing what they did best and jogged down the road. He found Declan's truck less than a tenth of a mile away. Mack had moved to the backseat of the king cab. Cole jumped in and leaned forward as they drove slowly along the road to the approximate location where he'd asked CJ to wait.

All the while, he prayed that his kiss hadn't scared her off, that she would be there. Based on her reaction to his kiss, she hadn't seemed angry. Just the opposite. She'd kissed him back. What worried him was why. Had she responded the way she had because she'd liked it? Or had she given him what he wanted with the intention of ditch-ing him and moving on by herself without raising his suspicion right away?

His breath lodged in his throat, Cole scanned the roadside, searching for the woman who'd captured his attention, his admiration and might just conquer his heart.

Chapter Five

CJ hunkered low in the shadows, watching the road, waiting for Cole, as she'd promised.

The CJ who'd been living on her own for the past year, remaining aloof and independent of anyone, itched to run and keep running. And she might have.

If not for that kiss.

Her lips still tingled and an ache she had never felt before built deep inside her.

Why had Cole kissed her? Did he think that would change anything?

She pressed her hand to her chest. It was so tight she could barely breathe. Was that a reaction to the kiss or the brush with death?

Vehicles lined up, close to the accident, their drivers waiting for the road to clear.

One by one, they moved through, the line shortening as law enforcement and firefighters cleared one lane of traffic.

A truck approached from the other direction, moving slowly. When it came within a hundred yards of her position, it stopped. The passenger door opened and a man got out. The light from the cab flashed on and then off as the door opened and closed.

CJ couldn't see who had climbed out or who was driving. She waited, sinking lower in the shadows.

"CJ?" Cole's voice called out.

Her heart skipped several beats and then slammed against her ribs, racing like a marathon runner's at the end of a course. She rose from her position and almost sprinted out into the road. Survival instincts kicked in and she stopped, looked around, searching the shadows for anyone hiding, waiting for her to come out. The men who'd come after her might only have moved down the road from the burning vehicle. They could be close, watching for her to relax and appear where they could easily pick her off.

"CJ?" Cole called again.

"I'm here," she responded, loud enough for him to hear.

"Keep talking." He headed in her direction. "Tell me when I'm getting warmer."

"You're getting warmer," she said, a smile pulling at her lips. She hadn't played hide-and-seek since she had been a little girl when her parents were still alive. The memory warmed her.

"Don't come out," Cole said, lowering his voice. "Let Declan bring the truck to us."

"I've no intention of presenting myself as a target," she said. "Keep coming."

When Cole was within range, she reached out and grabbed his arm, pulling him into the shadows with her.

"Thank God," he said and wrapped his arms around her.

She chuckled. "Did you think I'd run?"

He tipped her chin up and cupped her face with his hand. "Yes, I did."

She clucked her tongue, her pulse racing, her body on fire where it touched his. "So little faith in me," she said with forced lightness.

"So much understanding of your situation," he said softly. "You're alive because you relied on yourself and your instincts." He bent to touch his lips to hers and then raised his head. "I thought I'd scared you away."

"Me? Scared?" She gave a shaky laugh. She had been scared. Afraid of how she felt. Afraid of falling for someone and making him a bargaining chip Trinity could use to get to her.

Cole kissed her again. Hard this time. Then he stepped back. "Ready to make a run for it?"

No. She was ready for another real kiss. "I'm ready."

Cole pulled her against him, shielding her body with his. "Let's go."

Declan had moved the truck as close to the edge of the trees as he could.

Cole and CJ took off in an awkward jog toward the vehicle, Cole using his body as the first line of defense against any bullets that might be lobbed their way.

When they reached the truck, he yanked open the door and shoved her into the front passenger seat. "Stay on the floorboard," he said and jumped in behind her, slamming the door shut behind him.

CJ crouched, her arms on Cole's knees, her chin on his lap.

Declan shifted into gear and took off, spitting up gravel from the shoulder as he lurched onto the pavement.

They hadn't gone far when something pierced the back windshield and traveled through the cab and out the front windshield.

Declan cursed and slammed his foot down on the accelerator, launching the truck forward. He zigzagged across the road to make it harder for the shooter to get a bead on them. "Mack, Cole, get down!" Declan hunched over the steering wheel, keeping his head as low as possible.

Cole leaned over, covering CJ's head and shoulders with his broad frame.

Another bullet smacked the rear window.

Declan jerked the steering wheel, sending the truck careening to the left.

CJ held on to Cole's legs to keep from falling over.

Declan grunted and straightened the truck. "I think we're pulling away from them."

"I don't see a vehicle behind us," Mack said from the backseat.

"Then they were on the ground," Cole said. "They were using what appeared to be AR-15s. I doubt they could have hit us if they'd been in a vehicle."

"It won't take them long to catch up."

"Then we'll just have to stay ahead of them," Declan said, an edge to his voice. He maintained a breakneck speed, barreling down the highway.

Cole sat up and looked around. "Only about a mile to go to get to the gate." He pulled out his phone and hit some buttons.

CJ shifted to ease a cramp forming in her calf.

"Someone open the gate and be ready to close it immediately," Cole said into the phone. "We're coming in hot and might have a tail."

When he ended the call, he looked down at her. "Are you okay?"

CJ gave him a grimace. "I'm fine." She tilted

her head toward Declan. Blood dripped from his side onto the seat. "But your friend isn't."

Declan's face was pale and his knuckles were white on the steering wheel. "I'm fine," he said through gritted teeth. "We're almost there."

Cole ripped off his jacket and pulled his T-shirt over his head.

"Where were you hit?" he demanded.

"Doesn't matter. We can take care of it when we get to Charlie's."

"Where?" Cole snapped.

Declan's lips pressed into a tight line. "Right side, just below my ribs."

Cole leaned over and pressed his T-shirt against Declan's side.

Declan took his hand off the wheel for a second, to direct Cole's hand to the spot, and winced.

"You keep your hands on the wheel. I've got this," Cole said.

CJ knelt on the floor and leaned over the console. "Let me," she said.

She slipped her hand beneath Cole's and held the shirt in place, applying pressure to the wound.

Declan slowed the truck.

Cole put his hand around CJ's hip and held on as they turned and passed through an impressive iron gate.

As soon as they were through, the gate shut. Men holding AR-15s waved them past and turned to face the gate and any threat that might present itself.

Declan picked up speed, taking them along the winding road into the estate, coming to a stop in front of the Halverson mansion. Declan shifted into Park and leaned his head against the headrest. "I can take it from here," he said, reaching around to the wad of T-shirt soaked in his blood.

"The heck you can. I've got this until they get you out and someone else can take over." CJ maintained pressure on Declan's wound.

Charlie Halverson, her assistant Grace and her butler Roger Arnold hurried down the steps to the truck.

"We're going to need an ambulance. Declan caught a bullet," Cole said as he dismounted and came around the other side.

"Calling 9-1-1." Mack hit the numbers on his phone while climbing out of the back.

"Help me get him out," Cole said.

Arnold joined Cole as he opened the driver's door.

Grace stood behind them, her eyes wide, her face pale.

"I'll get blankets, towels and sheets." Charlie ran back inside.

Cole reached in, hooked Declan beneath his shoulders and dragged him across the seat and out of the cab.

"I can get myself out," Declan said through gritted teeth.

"Right," Cole grunted as he took the bulk of Declan's weight, looping his arm over his neck as the injured man stumbled down out of the vehicle.

Arnold slipped under Declan's other arm.

CJ scrambled across the seat and out to walk behind them, pressing the shirt against the wound in Declan's back.

Grace hurried up the stairs and opened the other side of the double doors, her face tight, her expression worried.

Guilt stabbed CJ in the heart. Declan was injured because the shooters were gunning for her. If the man died, it would be CJ's fault.

Collateral damage.

She shouldn't have gotten them involved. This was her battle. She should have fought it alone.

An overwhelming desire to turn around and run from here swamped her. But if she did that, she'd be abandoning them. They were in it with her, whether she wanted them now or not. She had to stay. To help. Just as they'd helped her.

Charlie met them in the front foyer. "Bring him into the sitting room. I spread sheets out over the sofa."

They carried Declan in and laid him on the sofa.

"You're making a big deal out of a little flesh

wound," Declan said. He grunted as they rolled him onto his stomach to better see the wound.

CJ shrugged out of her backpack, dropped it on the floor and pulled her knife out of the scabbard strapped to her leg.

Cole gripped the hem of Declan's shirt and held it tight.

CJ dug her knife into the fabric to cut an opening, then sheathed her knife and ripped the fabric up his back, exposing the bullet hole.

Grace gasped. "Oh, Declan."

"Grace, I'm all right," Declan said, his voice muffled against the sofa's cushion. He held out his hand.

Staying out of the way, Grace sank to her knees and held his hand. "Sure, babe. Just a flesh wound." A tear slipped from the corner of her eye. She glanced away. "Any news on that ambulance?"

"On its way," Mack confirmed. "ETA five minutes."

Arnold approached, folding a hand towel into a square. He placed it on the wound and applied pressure.

"Who's on the gate?" Cole asked.

"Mustang, Gus and Jack," Mack said.

"They know to check before they open the gate?" Cole asked.

"Roger," Mack said. "Just got off the phone with them."

CJ stood back, watching as the team rallied around their injured comrade. She wanted to help, but they had everything under control.

Her gaze met Cole's.

He stepped away from the sofa and captured her arm in his, drawing her with him out of the sitting room. "Are you all right?" he asked.

She nodded. "I'm fine. It's your friend who's injured. He wouldn't have been if I hadn't gotten into the truck."

Cole shook his head. "Did you shoot him?"

CJ's brow dipped. "No. But—"

"Then it's not your fault. Those men shot him."

"But—"

He pressed a finger to her lips, shaking his head slowly. "You don't have to do this alone anymore. We are going to help you."

"You don't understand," CJ said. "Trinity won't stop until I'm dead."

"Then we have to stop Trinity. That was our goal. Whether we'd met you or not." He smiled down at her. "You've already helped us once. You might as well stick with us."

"Are you speaking for everyone on your team?" CJ shook her head. "They might not agree."

"Your situation is exactly why we established Declan's Defenders," a voice said from behind Cole.

Cole turned to face Charlie Halverson and smiled. "Right. It's what we do."

Charlie smiled at CJ. "And until we stop Trinity, you can stay here."

"I can't impose on you," CJ said.

"Yes, you can. What's the use of having a big house if I can't share it?" She nodded to Cole. "And since you're assigned to help CJ, you'll stay, as well. If you want, I can show you to your rooms."

"If it's all the same to you," CJ said, "I want to wait until I know Declan will be okay."

As if on cue, Mack exited the room. "Fire truck, ambulance and two sheriffs' vehicles just passed through the gate."

Charlie spun and headed for the sitting room. "How's our patient?"

Mack followed. "Cranky."

"He has a right to be." Charlie's voice faded.

CJ started to follow.

Cole gripped her arm, his eyes narrowed. "So, you'll stay?"

Her lips tightening, CJ hesitated. She might be making a big mistake, but she nodded. "I'm staying."

Cole relaxed. "Good. It will be easier for me to help you, if I know where you are." They stood outside the door of the sitting room, staring in at Declan who was lying on the sofa, holding Grace's hand. "I'm not sure how you've managed to lie low, but I'm willing to bet it wasn't by talking to the police or sheriff's deputies."

She glanced out the window at the vehicles pulling up to the front of the estate. "True."

"You might want to disappear while they're here," Mack called out. "We'll avoid mentioning you as a passenger in the truck."

"Or the Hummer," Cole added.

Once again, they were putting their lives and integrity on the line for her.

Cole touched her arm. "Just go with it and get scarce."

CJ nodded. "Thank you."

Charlie led her to another room in the house that would allow her to watch without being spotted and questioned.

These people had gone above and beyond for her. No one had done that for her since…

She couldn't remember.

Her eyes stung and filled. She blinked hard, appalled at the sudden emotional response. Hadn't she learned anything from Trinity? Crying showed weakness. Never cry.

COLE HOVERED IN the massive entryway as the EMTs worked to stabilize Declan and load him into the ambulance. He kept a close watch on the door Charlie had led CJ through. He didn't trust her not to run. The woman was skittish and rightly so.

The same first responders who had been at the

scene of the Hummer fire were the ones who'd arrived in front of Charlie's home.

While Declan was being cared for, the law-enforcement professionals spent a lot of time examining the truck and asking questions of Cole and Mack.

The ambulance left for the hospital with Grace riding in the back, still holding Declan's hand.

What seemed like hours later, the sheriff's deputies departed.

CJ emerged into the foyer, joining Charlie, Mack, Roger Arnold and Cole.

"After two attacks, I think it would be best to maintain perimeter security for the night," Cole said.

"Arnold and I will help Charlie's security guards. Mustang, Walsh and Snow will cover the night perimeter," Mack said.

"I can pull night duty to relieve someone," Cole offered.

"That goes for me, as well," CJ said.

Mack shook his head. "We can only cover so much. If anyone gets by, Cole will be your only defense."

CJ stiffened. "I can defend myself."

"Which is a huge advantage," Cole said. "It means while I'm watching your six, you can be watching mine. We're a team, now. As a team, we look out for each other."

"That's right," Mack agreed.

"And we will also be Charlie's last line of defense," Cole added.

"With everyone but you and Cole on the gate and walls, I'll feel a lot better knowing I have two trained professionals watching out for me," Charlie said.

CJ slung her backpack over her shoulder.

Charlie took her hand. "Now, if you two will come with me, I'll show you where you can sleep."

Cole followed CJ and Charlie up the sweeping staircase to the second level.

"You can have the blue room, CJ, and Cole will be in the room beside you, should you need assistance." She opened the door and stepped inside. "There's a bathroom across the hall. I'll bring you something to sleep in, and I'll have your clothing cleaned and ready for you by morning."

"I don't want to be a bother," CJ said. "I have some things of my own. Although, nothing in the way of sleepwear."

Charlie laughed. "Just so you know, you're not the first one of our rescues to stay here. Grace and I have amassed a stash of clothing in different sizes. Seems we're getting people who come to us in similar circumstances. You know, on the run, with nothing but the clothes on their backs." Charlie's brow furrowed. "It's nothing to be ashamed of.

And we love to help. I would hope that if I find myself in a similar situation, someone will help me."

"Thank you," CJ said. For the second time in one day, that stinging feeling swept through her eyes and she blinked hard. She dropped her backpack on a chair.

"I'll be right back with those clothes." Charlie left CJ in the room with Cole.

"Are you all right?" Cole asked.

CJ blinked, squared her shoulders and faced him. "I'm perfectly fine."

He touched a hand to her cheek. "Then why are you crying?"

CJ batted his hand away from her cheek and wiped her hand across a damp spot, appalled that a tear had slipped out of her eye and made a trail down her face. "I don't cry," she said through gritted teeth. "I never cry."

"There's no dishonor in crying." Cole's fingers curled around her arms.

"There is if it's me."

Cole's jaw hardened. "Is that what you learned from Trinity?"

"I learned it even before Trinity, when they placed me in a foster home. No one cares about orphans. They're expendable. Like their parents."

"No, CJ. They aren't. Every child deserves to be loved and looked after."

She snorted and turned away. "You grew up in a different world than the one I grew up in."

"That doesn't make mine the only way to grow up," Cole said.

"Or mine wrong," CJ whispered. "Just different. And we learn to adapt to our environments."

Cole dipped his head. "Granted." He cupped her cheek again. "But you don't live in that world anymore."

"Don't I?" She stared up at him, her heart pinching hard in her chest. "Until Trinity is wiped off the face of this planet, I will never have another life. I will always be on the run, looking over my shoulder, expecting someone to shoot me in the back."

"You have me, now. I've got your back." He leaned close and kissed her cheek where the tear had been. "I promise to do my very best to keep you safe from harm." He kissed the other cheek.

"You don't understand Trinity," CJ murmured, her heart fluttering. "They're relentless."

With his thumb, he tipped her chin up. "I can be relentless, as well."

CJ shifted her gaze from his eyes to his lips. How she wanted him to press his mouth to hers. She could almost taste his lips. "It could take years to end their terror."

"I'm in this for the long haul." He lowered his head, his lips capturing hers.

For a long moment, he held her until footsteps echoed in the hallway.

Cole released her and stepped back as Charlie entered the room with an armload of clothing. "I forgot to ask you what size you wore, so I grabbed a few things in a couple different sizes."

Heat rose in CJ's cheeks. She held out her hands to take the pile. "Thank you. I'm sure I can find something that will work."

"If you'll leave the things you're wearing now outside the door, I'll have Roger collect them. We can have them cleaned and back to you by morning."

"Please, I can do my own laundry, if you point me to the washing machine," CJ said.

Charlie shook her head. "Roger won't let anyone touch the washer or dryer. He just replaced them with a fancy new set and insists on doing all the laundry. He lets others help fold, but he won't let anyone near the new machines." Charlie chuckled. "You'd never guess the man is former British Army."

CJ's eyes widened. "How did you get such a man to be your butler?"

Charlie shrugged. "My husband hired him. I think he was looking for a less dangerous position after he was injured and retired from the SAS, the Special Air Service, the Brits' special forces."

Cole snorted. "How's that working out for him?"

Charlie grinned. "Let's just say his skills as a butler are impeccable. But his skills from his SAS days have saved our butts on more than one occasion." She looked around the room. "If you need anything else, just ask me, Grace or Roger. Although, Grace will be at the hospital until Declan is released. Which, by the way, should be soon. I received word the bullet missed all the vital organs."

CJ drew in a deep breath and let it out in a long sigh. "I'm glad to hear that." A weight lifted off her chest and she breathed freely for the first time in a few hours.

"The doctor said he'll be fine as long as he doesn't get an infection. He's got Declan on antibiotics and pain medications." Charlie's lips thinned. "We have to find the people who are doing this and put a stop to their brand of terrorism."

CJ and Cole nodded.

Charlie's face lightened. "On that note, I'll leave you two to rest. Good night." The widow left them and walked to the far end of the hallway to her suite of rooms.

Once the door closed, Cole turned to CJ. "You need rest. If you need anything else, all you have to do is yell. I'll hear you."

"I'll be fine," CJ said. "I'm glad your teammate will be okay."

Cole shook his head, "It would take a lot more than a mere bullet to bring that man down." He smiled. "And that's not the first bullet he's caught." He crossed to the door. "You can have the shower first. I want to go check on a few things with Jonah."

Still holding the collection of clothing, CJ nodded. "Thank you for being there for me. I know it's your job, but I still appreciate it."

Cole's brow furrowed. "It's not just a job, CJ." He closed the distance between them, took the clothes from her hands and laid them on the bed. Then he cupped her cheeks in his hands. "It's more than the job. I kinda like you." Then he kissed her hard, his mouth descending on hers, taking and coaxing her to give back.

She gasped, her lips opening to him, allowing him to sweep in and kiss her like their tomorrows were uncertain.

When he finally raised his head, he stepped back, his hands falling to his sides. "You have every right to slap my face. And I encourage you to do so, if you don't want me to do that again."

She pressed a hand to her throbbing lips, her tongue tied and her voice lodged in her throat.

"Now, I have to go before I do something we

might both regret." He spun on his heels and left the room, closing the door behind him.

CJ should have been relieved, but she couldn't help wondering what he might regret doing. Her only regret at the moment was that he didn't do whatever it was.

Chapter Six

Cole fought the desire to stay with CJ, pick her up and toss her on the bed. Then he'd make sweet love to her through the night.

He adjusted his jeans, without hope of loosening the tight constraints. Time would accomplish that. Or a cold shower.

He needed to meet with Jonah to see if the young computer geek had any information for them to go on. They had been operating in the dark for far too long.

Any one of them could have taken that bullet. Mack, who'd been seated in the backseat, had been lucky it hadn't hit him.

Cole descended the staircase, the taste of CJ's mouth lingering in his. She was so tempting. And he'd been wrong to take advantage of her when she'd been through so much over the past year. Hell, over her entire life. She didn't need a man coming on to her. She'd had enough men in her life telling her what to do and when to do it. She deserved to make her own decisions, not have him forcing one on her.

But then, she hadn't fought him. In fact, she'd kissed him back. But was that because she'd wanted to? Or had she gone along with him because that was what was expected?

Cole could have kicked himself for succumbing so easily to his desires without taking CJ's wants and needs into consideration.

Bottom line, he had to keep his hands and lips to himself.

Jonah was in the war room beneath John Halverson's old study, tapping away on his computer keyboard.

Cole sat at the computer beside his and clicked the mouse to bring the computer to life. "Anything new?" he asked, hoping and praying for a fresh lead. Anything that could steer them in the right direction. They'd had so little to go on so far.

"I got word that the FBI and Secret Service investigators followed up with Chris Carpenter about the text message he sent to Tully before the attack. Carpenter swears he didn't even have his cell on him that morning. He'd left it at home."

"Interesting," Cole muttered. "If he didn't send the text, who sent it for him?"

"It might be worth tapping into his computer at home to see if we can find anything, but he doesn't leave it on or tied into the internet when he's not at home," Jonah said. "I've tried for the past few hours and, apparently, he doesn't log on very often. There's a limit to what we can get from here. We need to send someone in to do a download of everything on his hard drive."

"What about his desktop at work?"

"It might be worth getting into, but he has it secured with a password and government common access card. It would take me a lot more time to hack into it than it would to send someone in to swipe his card and access it while he's away from his desk."

"Can you get me and CJ inside the West Wing like you did for Snow when he went to work for Anne as her assistant?"

Jonah grinned. "Already have you and CJ in their system. You as yourself and CJ as Charlotte Jones. All I need are pictures to go on the cards and you're golden." He tilted his head toward the camera behind him. "If you'll stand in front of the camera, I'll get yours ready right now."

"I can have CJ come down after she showers so that you can take her picture."

Jonah nodded.

"I can do it now," a voice said from behind them.

Cole turned to find CJ standing at the bottom of the staircase leading into the basement war room.

"I thought you would be in the shower."

She shrugged. "I needed a drink of water. When I came downstairs, I heard your voice and came to see if you'd learned anything else."

"Well, good. We can take care of this now." Jonah stood and stepped behind the camera.

"Aren't you concerned someone might recognize you?" Cole said. "We got some of the Trinity sleepers who'd been working at the White House. There could be more."

CJ raised a single finger. "Hold that thought." She turned and ran up the stairs.

Cole could hear her footsteps ascending the staircase, moving quickly. Then they were coming down again and CJ entered the war room, her backpack in her hands. She placed it on the conference table in the middle of the room and rummaged inside.

A moment later, she pulled out a black wig and a blond wig and held them up. "Which would be more appropriate for the office?"

"Blond," Jonah said at the same time Cole said, "Black."

CJ's brow furrowed. "Seriously?"

Cole frowned at Jonah and then faced CJ. "You'll be a little more invisible with the black wig."

"Then black it is." She pulled her auburn hair up and secured it in a ponytail that she then wrapped around the base several times, securing it in place using pins. Tipping her head down, she pulled the wig over her scalp and tucked in any stray strands of dark red hair.

Straightening, she slipped a pair of black-framed glasses onto her nose. The transformation was uncanny.

Jonah chuckled. "Perfect."

Her costume didn't make CJ any less desirable in Cole's books. In fact, it made him want her even more. Though CJ was a knockout with black hair and those thick, black-framed glasses, Cole wanted to tear them off her and reveal the beautiful woman she was beneath. She shouldn't have to disguise who she really was.

"If you'll step in front of the camera, I'll get this ID card made for you. I've set you up as Chris Carpenter's temporary assistant. You'll be filling in for Dr. Millicent Saunders until she's back from medical leave."

"The woman who was run down over a week ago by Trinity," Cole confirmed.

Jonah nodded. "I understand she'll be out on convalescent leave for a couple more weeks. Cole is coming in as tech support to manage a work order Carpenter put to have his office rearranged, moving his desk, phone and computer to a different wall."

"A worker out to move his stuff?" CJ asked.

"He put in the request over a month ago. I imagine it's been low on their priority list," Jonah said.

"You sure we'll get in with these cards?" CJ stood in front of the camera and waited for Jonah to snap the picture.

"I got Jack Snow in, I can get you in," Jonah said.

"Remind me not to make you mad at me," Cole murmured.

"I can get you in, but you'll have to figure out how to get a backup of Carpenter's hard drive without him catching on to you."

"We'll get Anne and Jack to show us the ropes," Cole said.

"I'll have the kinks worked out by the time you leave for work in the morning." Jonah clicked on the computer and waited while the information and image imprinted on the card. When it was done, he handed the card to CJ. "Run it through the scanner." He tipped his head toward the card reader set up in the corner of the room. "It should work the same at the West Wing. I'll also create a Virginia driver's license matching your assumed name—in case the Secret Service question you. Anne said they've tightened security since she and the VP were involved in that foiled kidnapping."

"Great." Cole shook his head. "What are the chances we'll have our cover blown before we even get inside?"

"One in ten?" Jonah quipped.

"Odds aren't all that great," Cole said, digging into a drawer and pulling out two tiny, flat, round disks. He held them up. "These look like watch batteries. We need to drop one into Carpenter's pocket. That way, we can track where he goes. He might lead us to whomever is pulling his strings, if in fact he's one of Trinity's agents. Even if he isn't part of Trinity, they might be using him to get what they want."

Cole glanced over at CJ.

She didn't look convinced about their ability to get inside the West Wing.

"I can get Anne Bellamy to help me get into Chris's office. You don't need to go."

"What excuse will Anne have to be in his office?" CJ shook her head. "No, I need to go. As a temporary replacement for Dr. Saunders, I would have more reason to be in Carpenter's office than Anne would. No use in her getting caught snooping. If I lose my job there, it's no big deal. I'm only a temporary employee."

"Like I said," Jonah interjected. "I'll have all this squared away by morning, and I'll have Cole with administrative authority to get onto Carpenter's computer." He waved them away. "Go on. Get some sleep."

"What about you?" Cole asked.

"I can sleep tomorrow. You two need this by

morning. I'll have it ready." Already, Jonah was back at his computer, his fingers flying over the keyboard.

CJ removed the wig and stuffed it into her backpack along with the black-framed glasses. "Thankfully, Charlie had a skirt, a white blouse and some black pumps in the stack of clothing. Hopefully, it'll be sufficient business attire for the job."

"I'm sure it will be." Cole took CJ's elbow. "We'd better leave the man to his work." He led her up the stairs and turned toward the kitchen instead of the staircase. "I could use a drink and something to eat."

CJ's stomach rumbled. "I hadn't realized that I haven't eaten since breakfast."

Cole shook his head. "Come to think of it, neither have I. Let's see what Charlie's chef left in the refrigerator. Carl's one of the best cooks the Navy let get away."

He opened one side of the double-door refrigerator. "I think we hit the jackpot." He pulled out a glass platter filled with slices of ham. "Care for a ham and cheese sandwich?"

"I'd love one." CJ pressed a hand to her belly. "Know where I can find plates?"

Together they unearthed condiments, plates and a knife. Minutes later, they had two thick ham sandwiches lying on plates and two glasses of milk.

"And I thought I was the only one who liked milk with my sandwich." He grinned.

"I'm all for strong bones. A big glass of milk with my sandwich is one of the few memories I have from my childhood before I went to train at Trinity." She took a bite and closed her eyes, a moan rising up her throat.

Cole's groin tightened. "You need to stop that right now," he said through gritted teeth.

Her eyes opened and widened. "Stop what?"

"Never mind." Cole focused on his sandwich and milk, refusing to look up at CJ. The woman was making him nuts. He finished his sandwich and milk and was surprised to see that CJ had finished hers as quickly. They rinsed their plates and glasses and placed them in the dishwasher.

Back at the top of the stairs, Cole walked CJ to her door and waited while she entered before he headed for his own room.

"Cole," CJ called out.

Cole turned, his pulse picking up. He wanted so badly to take CJ into his arms and hold her. He couldn't understand how he'd come to this point so quickly with a woman he'd known only a short time.

She stared at him for a long moment. "Why did you kiss me?"

He closed his eyes, drew in a deep, calming breath and let out it before opening his eyes again. "To tell the truth… I don't know. I can't seem to stop myself."

CJ's eyes flared and her tongue swept across her lips. "Are you sorry you did it?"

His gaze captured hers. "Are you?" He held his breath, wanting to know the truth but afraid of her response.

UNSURE OF THIS mating game people played, CJ finally shook her head. "No, I'm not sorry you did it." In a lower voice, she continued. "I'm only sorry you won't do it again."

Cole crossed the floor, pulled her into his arms and kissed her before the last consonant rolled off her tongue. He crushed her mouth with his in a soul-capturing kiss that rocked her to her very core.

When he finally allowed her to breathe again, he pressed his forehead to hers. "I can't keep doing this."

"Why not?" she asked.

"Because, the more I do it, the more I want."

Her heart fluttered, an unusual feeling to the hardened warrior inside her. "That's funny," she said with a little laugh.

"Why is it funny?" he asked, pulling back to look into her eyes.

She met his gaze unflinchingly. "Because that's exactly how I feel." CJ reached around him and gave the door a gentle push, letting it swing shut behind Cole. Her breath hitched as she made a decision. "Don't go. Please."

"Are you sure this is what you want?" Cole shoved a hand through his hair. "I can leave now. But if I stay, I'll want much more than just a kiss. Tell me to leave now."

CJ grabbed his hand and brought it to her lips. "I need a shower after rolling around in the woods." Her lips curled upward on the corners.

"So do I."

"Care to join me?" she asked, her voice thick and gravelly, strange to her own ears.

Cole pulled her close to him, again in a long, passionate kiss.

When he tore his mouth away, he scooped her up in his arms. "A shower for my lady," he said and kissed the tip of her nose.

With his hands full, he couldn't maneuver the door handle.

CJ reached out, twisted it and pulled it open.

Cole carried her through and across the hallway to the bathroom where he set her on her feet.

Grabbing the hem of her shirt, CJ pulled it up over her head and let it fall to the floor. Then she gripped his T-shirt and tugged it up his torso, stopping halfway up.

Apparently impatient to get naked, Cole tore his shirt the rest of the way off and tossed it into a corner.

CJ reached behind her back for the clasp to her bra.

Cole brushed her hands away and fumbled with the hooks, releasing them and sliding the straps slowly over her shoulders and down her arms. As he did so, her breasts fell free of the garment.

With her breath arrested in her lungs, she fought to draw more in. As her chest rose, so, too, did her breasts, into Cole's cupped palms.

How warm and rough they were against her nipples. Sweet abrasion that made the heat rise low in her belly and her center ache for more.

He trailed kisses from the corner of her mouth down the long line of her neck and over her collarbone.

"I'm not very good at this," she admitted, her voice breathy, her hands spanning his hard chest, touching the smooth planes, reveling in the strength of his muscles beneath her fingertips. She had to see more, feel more, and press her body to his in all the right places.

CJ undid the drawstring of her sweatpants, kicked off her shoes and pushed her sweats down her legs, stepping free.

Cole reached into the shower stall and turned on the water. When it had warmed, he finished undressing, toeing off his boots and shucking off his jeans. When he stood naked in front of CJ, she had trouble breathing.

The man was beautiful from the shock of dark hair to the tips of his toes. His broad shoulders seemed to fill the bathroom.

He took her hand and stepped into the shower, ducking beneath the spray, letting the water run over his head and shoulders and across his chest. When he was good and wet, he turned and let her stand beneath the spray.

A shower had always been a means of cleansing her body, nothing more.

Cole showed CJ how much more a shower could be. That it could be a gentle ministration, something tender and sexy at the same time. He lathered a bar of soap in his hands and rubbed the suds over her shoulders and along the long, smooth line of her arms. Then he captured her hips in his soapy hands and followed the curve of her waist up to cup her breasts in his palms.

CJ sucked in a sharp breath, the movement pressing her breasts more firmly into his hands.

He thumbed her nipples and circled them, again and again, the suds washing free of her skin as the spray sluiced over her body. Then he bent to take one of them in his mouth, sucking gently on the little rosy-brown bud. Flicking it with his tongue, he had her so worked up she could barely breathe.

Cole cupped the backs of her thighs and lifted her, pressing her against the cool tile. "You're driving me crazy."

"That's my line," she said, kissing the droplets off his forehead. She wrapped her legs around his waist and sank down until the tip of his shaft nudged her entrance.

He closed his eyes, as if he was in pain, and then opened them again. "Not yet."

He set her on her feet, poured shampoo into his hands and lathered her hair.

CJ had never had a man wash her hair. His hands were gentle, and he kissed her often before he turned her back to the water, tipped her head beneath the spray and rinsed the suds from her strands.

Then he lathered his hands again and smoothed them over her entire body from the back of her neck to the tips of her toes, slowing to dip his fingers inside her, making her legs shake and her entrance slick with more than soap.

When Cole was done, CJ took over, lathering his body, exploring every square inch of skin. When she came to his jutting erection, she circled it with both hands and slid her fingers up and down, loving the contrast of the velvety softness of the skin encasing his hardness. She knelt in the shower's spray and took him into her mouth, tonguing the tip and then tracing a circle around the circumference.

Cole's body tensed and his fingers dug into her hair, holding her close. When she took all of him into her mouth, he sucked in a breath and held it.

She leaned back, letting him out almost all of the way before taking him in again.

Settling into a rhythm, she sucked him in and out until his fingers dug into her scalp and he pushed her away.

"Too close," he said through gritted teeth.

She shook her head, a smile curling her lips. "Never." When she tried to take him again, he pulled her to her feet and set her outside the shower on the bath mat. "We're done here."

She blinked the water from her eyes, a frown pulling her brow downward. "Done?" No way. She wanted so much more.

"Done. Here." He nodded toward the shower as he stepped out beside her on the bath mat. With quick, efficient movements, he toweled her dry.

Using a big, fluffy towel, CJ returned the favor, lingering over that prominent protrusion, her body on fire, begging to consummate their time together. She might never have this kind of opportunity again. Being from completely different backgrounds, what were the chances that what they were feeling and doing would last more than a night, maybe two? She'd take whatever she could get and save the memories for when she was alone once again.

Once they were dry, Cole wrapped a towel around his waist and one around CJ's body. Then he scooped CJ up into his arms and strode toward the door.

She reached down to twist the knob, open the door and peer out. "Coast is clear."

Cole strode across the hallway, nudged open the door to her bedroom and carried her over the threshold. He didn't slow until he reached the bed. He set her on her feet and backed her up until her knees bumped into the mattress and she sat.

"Don't move." Cole stepped away from her and rummaged in the nightstand. When he didn't find what he was looking for, he left the room and returned to the bathroom.

CJ leaned over, her gaze following him through the door until he disappeared. She held the towel up over her breasts, her body on fire, barely cooling, even after he left her alone.

Cole was back in moments, carrying his jeans, pulling his wallet from the back pocket. He dug into the folds and pulled out a small foil package with a triumphant grin.

"I'm glad someone is thinking." CJ stood and took the packet from his fingers. At the same time, she let the towel slide down her body to pool at her feet. "Now, where were we?"

Cole jerked the towel free from his hips and sent it sailing across the room. "I think we were about to rock the world."

She tore open the packet and slid the protection over his engorged shaft. Backing up to the bed, she sat and scooted backward across the mattress.

Following, Cole climbed up onto the bed, settled between her legs and leaned over her. His staff nudged her opening.

CJ let her knees fall to the side, ready to take him into her.

Cole hesitated, bending to claim her lips. "Not yet," he repeated.

"Seriously?" she said, her voice a breathy whisper. "I want you. Now."

"I promise. I'll get there. But first…" He trailed kisses along her jaw and down the length of her neck. When he reached her breasts, he cupped one while he tongued, nipped and licked the tip of the other. When the nipple tightened into a hard bead, he moved to the other breast and gave it the same treatment.

CJ's blood hummed through her veins, molten hot. Heat coiled at her core, her body willing him to take her. But he wasn't ready.

Cole worked his way down her torso to the triangle of hair covering her sex. He paused, parted her folds and blew a warm stream of air over that special place. Without giving her time to breathe, he thumbed that nubbin of flesh and replaced his thumb with his tongue, tapping, flicking and laving her until she writhed beneath him.

When she thought she couldn't take any more, he flicked her again, sending her shooting over the edge. She arched her back, digging her heels into the mattress. Her channel throbbed with the intensity of the sensations splintering through her.

What seemed like seconds later, she fell back to earth, her need still strong, her desire to have Cole washing over her. All of Cole. Inside her. Now.

She laced her fingers into his hair and dragged him up her body.

"Hey, the hair is attached," he said, chuckling as he leaned over her, his gaze capturing hers. "Ready?"

"What do you think?" she quipped as she gripped his buttocks and guided him home.

He sank into her, moving slowly, letting her adjust to his girth. When he'd gone as far as he could, he pulled back out and started all over again.

The pace was far too slow for CJ. She wanted all of him, hard, fast and completely. Her hands still on his buttocks, she set the rhythm, showing him how she wanted it.

He complied, taking over to the point she let her hands fall to her sides where she curled them into the comforter and raised her hips to meet him thrust for thrust.

Cole moved in and out of her, pumping hard, his face tight, his body tense. After one last thrust, he buried himself to the hilt and held steady, his shaft throbbing against the walls of her channel.

A few moments later, he collapsed on top of her and rolled her onto her side, maintaining their intimate connection.

Cole draped a hand over her bare hip and sighed. "I didn't intend to make love to you," he said.

"And now that you have?" she asked, holding her breath for his answer, sure he'd say he wished he hadn't.

"Now that I have, I don't know how I'll keep from doing it again." He leaned close to her and pressed a kiss to her lips. "You are amazing."

CJ let out the breath she'd been holding and laughed. "You're not so bad yourself."

"What are we going to do now?" he asked.

"What do you mean?" CJ asked. "Just because we had sex, doesn't change anything."

A frown dented Cole's brow. "The hell it doesn't. It changes everything."

"How so?"

"I'm thinking, since I'm too involved in you, I might lose my situational awareness." He cupped her cheek. "I might not be the right person to protect you."

CJ stiffened in his arms. "Are you trying to quit on me?"

"I don't want to, but how can I provide your protection when all I want to do is make love to you again?"

"I never said I needed protection," she reminded him.

"But you know, as well as I, that you do need someone to have your six."

"Let me put it this way. I don't want anyone providing my protection—which I don't need—unless it's you." She frowned across at him. "Unless you're trying to break it off with me. If that's the case, you don't have to come up with any excuses. You can just leave."

She held up her hand to cut off his next words. That stinging sensation burned her eyes. CJ held tightly to her emotions. "And don't worry, you won't break my heart. I never had one to begin with."

It was a lie. If she didn't have a heart, why the hell did it feel like it was cracking…right down the middle?

Chapter Seven

Cole lay for a long time after CJ went to sleep, going over her words in his mind. The woman was delusional. *Never had a heart to begin with?* That was horse hockey. The woman had more heart than even she knew. When they'd first encountered her and learned of her defection from Trinity, she'd told them the triggering event had been her assignment to kill a pregnant woman. The fact that she couldn't pull the trigger on the woman and her unborn baby said it all. And she'd risked her own safety, coming out of hiding to alert Anne Bellamy to an attack on the White House.

The woman cared more than she would admit. And he'd be a real bastard to think he could make love to her and walk away.

CJ had been left behind as a child, sucked into a killer organization at a young age and given little to no love. That she cared enough to help others was amazing in itself. One didn't learn that in the environment where she'd been raised. That kind of compassion was as much a part of her as the color of her glorious auburn hair.

Cole stared at her in the little bit of starlight making its way through the windows into the bedroom. He'd been right, telling her that he was the wrong man for the job of protecting her. With her around, he'd have a hard time concentrating on the little clues that might pop up. His attention would be on her and his mind on what he could be doing with her behind closed doors.

If he wanted to remain her protector, he had to be careful and retain his focus. No matter what, he couldn't let anyone slide through his defenses and get to her. All it took was one well-aimed bullet to end her life.

Though Cole hadn't known her for long, he realized he wanted to know her even more. One night of making love to the strong, determined woman could not be the end. He wouldn't let it be. But until they captured the head of Trinity, they would all have to be looking out for each other and their special guest.

The thought of letting someone else take over her protection was enough to kill him. If he couldn't be with her every moment of every day, he'd be worried and on edge. No. He'd force himself to keep his eyes open and stay alert. He had to be the one to cover her six. He wouldn't hesitate to take a bullet for her.

He must have fallen asleep because the next thing he remembered was the blaring of the alarm clock on the nightstand beside CJ's bed.

CJ slapped the alarm, killing the irritating sound. She leaned up on one arm and stared down at him, the sheet falling away from a bare breast.

Cole blinked open his eyes and smiled. "You look like a Valkyrie lording it over your conquest."

"I feel like one." She sat up and stretched her long arms over her head. When she brought her arms down, she turned and snuggled back into his embrace, resting a hand across his chest. "Do we have to sneak into the West Wing today?"

"I'd much rather stay here with you." Cole brushed a strand of her hair from her cheek. "Can we put it off for another day?"

"Though I love the feeling of your hands on my skin, I know we can't wait another day to take down Trinity." Her fingernails curled into Cole's flesh. "I wish Trinity didn't exist. Then things could have been different between us. I could spend all day with you, just like this."

"If Trinity didn't exist, we might never have met," he pointed out. "For that reason alone, I'm glad they exist. Not that I'm glad you were recruited, but...you know what I mean."

She nodded. "Still, I'd rather stay here with you."

"If it's any consolation to you and me, I'll be with you all day." He gave her a lopsided grin. "Albeit, fully clothed and hands-off."

CJ snorted. "Not the same," she said, twirling a finger around one of his little brown nipples, tickling him. "I guess we don't have time to... you know."

Cole turned on his side and ran a hand over her shoulder, cupped a breast and tweaked her nipple between his thumb and forefinger.

She gasped, her body arching toward him.

"We can't go all the way there without protection, but that doesn't mean we can't have a little fun." He traced a line down her torso to the juncture of her thighs.

CJ shifted, parting her legs, letting him in to strum that little nubbin of tightly packed nerves.

She closed her eyes and let his fingers do all the talking, flicking, tapping and dipping into her channel for the warm juices that made his digits slide across that sensitive spot.

Before long, he had her poised on the edge, her body tense, her hips rocking to his tender ministrations. One more flick and she stiffened, her body rising up to meet his hand. He continued touching her there until she sank back to the mattress, her body limp, glistening with a fine sheen of perspiration.

Cole leaned over and kissed her, drawing her into his arms, pressing his engorged staff against her belly. He wanted more, but he didn't have anything left in his wallet. No protection. No making love.

CJ wrapped her fingers around him and moved up and down the shaft.

His breath caught and held. He could let her do what she was doing, but he'd want to take it to the next level. Instead, he captured her hand in his and held it still, shaking his head. "We have to get ready for work."

"But I want you to feel what I felt," she whispered.

"I did," he said. "Through you." He smacked her bottom and sat up. "Come on, we have some undercover work to do. The sooner we catch Trinity's leader, the sooner we can laze around in bed doing what we like doing better."

Cole rose, wrapped a towel around his waist and leaned down to capture her mouth in one last kiss. Then he was out the door, leaving her to dress and prepare for a day at the West Wing, gathering information about Chris Carpenter's role in the attack. That is, if in fact he had a part in the kidnapping of the vice president.

Grabbing his toiletries, he headed to the bathroom to shave. He returned to his bedroom, dressed in his only suit and tie. When he was ready, he fully expected to have to wait for CJ. Opening his bedroom door, he was surprised to see CJ standing there wearing a simple black skirt, a white blouse and black pumps on her feet. She'd tucked her gorgeous auburn hair up into the black wig and had on her black-framed glasses with the clear lenses. Even in the supposedly frumpy disguise, she was sexy as hell.

Cole pulled her into his arms and kissed her hard.

She opened to him and he slid his tongue along hers in a caress he didn't want to end.

When it did, he stood back and ran his gaze over her from top to toe. "You look amazing."

"I didn't think you could look better than when you wore your jeans and a T-shirt. But this look?" She nodded. "Sexy as hell."

He held out his elbow. "Ready to conquer the world?"

"I am." She slipped her hand through the bend of his elbow and walked with him down the staircase to the ground floor.

Cole led her toward the voices he heard coming from the kitchen.

Mustang, Charlie, Anne, Jack, Jonah and Carl the chef were busy setting the table, toasting bread and pouring coffee and orange juice into mugs and glasses.

They all settled at the table and discussed the day ahead.

Anne gave them a brief description of the layout of the offices in the West Wing and where they could find Chris Carpenter's.

"I put together a small tool kit for you to use when you move Carpenter's desk around," Jonah said. "Nothing in the kit should raise any alarms with the guards at the entrance. I even packed several types of batteries so that the two GPS disks will look like any other small, flat batteries. I also gave you the printout of the work order."

"Thank you." Cole scooped fluffy scrambled eggs onto his plate and a couple of slices of crispy bacon.

"It would be better if you and CJ don't show up at the West Wing at the same time." Mustang held up a hand. "Don't worry. Anne and Jack can walk her in to make certain she isn't targeted."

Cole frowned. "I don't like being that far away from her. She's my assignment."

CJ stiffened beside him, making him realize how callous his words sounded.

"I mean, I want to be the one to protect her." He turned to CJ. "I've been with you the longest."

"I can manage getting into the West Wing without a bodyguard," CJ said. "For that matter, it might be better if I don't get too close to any of you. Trinity is likely to know by now that you're all working together to bring them down."

"She has a point," Charlie said.

"In which case," Mustang said, "since I'm not one of the people going to work in the White House, I could wear a disguise and go with CJ as far as the entrance to the West Wing."

Cole didn't like the idea of being separated from CJ for even a minute, but they were right. Trinity had to be watching Charlie's estate by now and anyone coming and going. He nodded. "We'll have to take separate vehicles to the train station."

"I'll drive CJ all the way in and let her off near the Capitol," Arnold said as he joined them at the table.

"I can catch the train, change shirts in a bathroom and put on a ball cap before I get off at Farragut station," Mustang said. "I can position myself at a crosswalk, where you can drop off CJ, and walk near her the rest of the way to the West Wing."

The more complicated the plan got, the less Cole liked it. "I'll be there as soon as I can get there by metro," he said. "Wait for me to do any snooping around."

CJ dipped her head. "I'll get in and check Carpenter's schedule and let you know via the burner phone what times he'll be out of office. You can schedule your work order around him leaving for a meeting." She frowned. "You can give me one of the GPS devices. I can slip it into his jacket, since I'll be with him all day."

Cole nodded. "I'll do that after I get the tool bag through security."

With plans in place, they finished breakfast and loaded up into separate vehicles. Mack and Gus arrived by the time they were ready to leave and tightened up the convoy of vehicles heading for the metro and DC.

CJ rode with Cole as far as the metro station.

"I'll see you soon," Cole said. "I'd rather be with you, but Mustang will take good care of you."

CJ opened her mouth, but Cole pressed a finger to her lips with a smile. "I know. You can take care of yourself. But it's nice to have backup." He squeezed her hand before he got out and boarded the train.

Anne, Jack Snow and Mustang arrived in separate vehicles. They got onto different train cars without acknowledging each other's presence. As far as curious onlookers could tell, they didn't know each other. And by watching the rearview mirror and looking behind their little caravan, Cole had determined that no one seemed to have followed them from Charlie's estate. But they couldn't take any chances. Trinity had an entire network of individuals swarming all over DC and surrounding areas.

Cole found a seat and studied the people on board, wondering if one or more of them worked for Trinity. How could he tell? The Trinity sleepers who'd been inside the West Wing looked like everyone else who worked there. It was impossible to tell the difference.

He prayed CJ's disguise was sufficient to get her in and keep her safe until he arrived.

Chapter Eight

CJ sat in the back of the SUV, relying on Roger Arnold to get her through the heavy morning DC traffic. Thankfully, they'd left far earlier than most and missed a significant portion of rush hour until they neared the heart of the political scene. By the time they'd arrived at the agreed upon drop-off point, the traffic had slowed to a crawl. In some places, it was more stop-and-go than a crawl.

Mustang stood at a bus stop not far from where CJ got out of the car. He wore an Atlanta Braves baseball cap and a light gray sweatshirt. CJ walked past him headed toward the White House. In her peripheral vision, she saw Mustang fall in behind her. Moving with purpose, she didn't take long to reach the West Wing of the White House.

As predicted, the security was still tight following the attack and subsequent kidnapping of the vice president and one of the mid-level staffers.

CJ still felt responsible for getting Anne Bellamy involved in that mess. But when she'd learned that John Halverson had asked Anne to spy on people in the White House, looking for anyone who might have connections to Trinity, CJ had reached out to her. She had seen mentions of a potential attack on the White House and had felt obligated to warn someone on the inside to be aware and safe.

What she hadn't expected was for Anne to be kidnapped along with the VP and used as leverage to lure CJ out of her hiding as a trade for the lives of Anne and the vice president.

She'd offered to make that trade to free two innocent people. But Declan's Defenders had had other plans. With her help, they'd brought down the Trinity sleeper agents, freed Anne and the VP and saved the day without bringing CJ out in the open.

She owed them a lot for their sacrifices and the risks they'd taken to rescue the hostages. They had been right in assuming a trade would accomplish little. Trinity wasn't known to leave anyone alive to identify their agents in a lineup. Had they made the trade, CJ, Anne and the VP would have died.

Using the information Anne had provided about entry and location of offices, CJ stepped through the doors, scanned her card and proceeded through the metal detectors. The card worked, the metal detectors didn't find anything amiss, and she was on her way into the West Wing.

One hurdle crossed, on to the next. She found the office of the Homeland Security Advisor, Chris Carpenter, pasted a smile on her face and entered.

Having seen several pictures of the man, CJ recognized Carpenter at once. He stood in the middle of the front office, waving a stack of papers at some poor woman.

"How am I supposed to get anything done without help?" he asked.

"I'm only on loan until they bring in a temp to replace Dr. Saunders," the woman said. "I have work to do in my other office, as well. I can't do everything."

CJ cleared her throat to gain their attention. "Are you Mr. Carpenter?" she asked, knowing the answer before he gave it.

"Yeah. Who are you?"

"HR sent me as a temporary replacement for Dr. Saunders."

"Oh, thank goodness," the other woman said and rushed for the door.

CJ held out her hand to the man standing in the middle of the room. "Charlotte Jones. You must be Chris Carpenter, my new boss for the time being."

He gripped her hand absently and gave it a

brief shake. "Can you type? Ever done any fact checking?"

CJ nodded. "Both."

"Are you even set up on the computer network?" Carpenter shook his head. "I don't know why they send me replacements when we have to spend the next two weeks getting them up and running on the server. By that time, Dr. Saunders will be back from sick leave."

"Let me see what I can do before we get tech services involved," CJ said. "Where will I be sitting?"

"You'll have to sit at Dr. Saunders's desk. And, speaking of tech services, they'll be in today to rearrange the connections in my office. And about damned time. I'll be out most of the morning and early afternoon to meetings. You'll have to familiarize yourself with the office on your own." He stared down at the papers in his hands. "These will have to suffice until I can make the changes." With one last glance, he headed for the door. "I'll be back before the end of the day."

After Carpenter left the office, CJ sat at the desk he'd indicated and tapped the mouse. The screen came to life. She stuck her access card into the reader on the computer base unit and entered the password Jonah had set up for her. Like magic, the computer came to life and let her into the server used by the staff of the West

Wing. Once there, she sifted through various files searching for ones created by Chris Carpenter.

None of the files on Dr. Saunders's computer provided any information, clues on the attack, a connection to Tully or the Trinity sleeper agent, posing as a Secret Service agent who'd set off the explosion. But then, CJ hadn't expected to find anything obvious. She needed to get onto Carpenter's computer to see if there were any files or emails stored there that could lead them to the man in charge of Trinity.

Until Cole arrived, she didn't dare walk into Carpenter's office or log on to his desktop computer. Having a representative from technical services gave her a good excuse to be in the Homeland Security Advisor's office. Or better yet, she would be the first line of defense should people want to go into Carpenter's office. She could waylay them with the news Chris was in meetings all day. At the same time, she could warn Cole someone was outside the door.

He only had to have enough private time to download the contents of the computer onto a portable hard drive. Then he'd make the adjustments to the office as requested, to the best of his ability, and get the heck out before anyone discovered he wasn't really part of the tech services team.

CJ spent the first half hour using the bug sweep device Jonah had given her to check the entire outer office for any signs of hidden cameras or microphones. When she was certain there weren't any, she carried a document into Carpenter's office, leaving the door open in case someone walked in. She had the excuse of leaving the document on his desk as the reason for being caught in his office.

The bug scanner came up empty. With both offices clear, she felt more confident Cole would be able to do what he had to do without being observed.

With nothing else to do to pass time, CJ studied the data pertaining to the Department of Homeland Security. She received emails from Carpenter giving her a list of tasks to accomplish by the time he returned to the office that afternoon.

CJ wasn't sure what she was supposed to do with some of the items on the list, but she gave it her best shot. Thankfully, Trinity had insisted all of the children placed in their hands be educated in math, the sciences, English and foreign languages. What she didn't know, she searched on the internet for information.

By the time Cole appeared, she was ready to get on with the work they'd come to do. And seeing him again brought back memories of their night together. Her body warmed.

"I've checked the offices for bugs," she said in a low voice. Though she'd checked, she still didn't fully trust that the device she'd used was fail proof. In a louder voice, she asked, "Are you the technical services representative here to move Mr. Carpenter's office around?"

"I am." Cole waved the work order in his hand. "Point me in the right direction and I'll get to it."

She led him to Carpenter's office, opened the door and let him in. "I take it you know what has to be done?"

He nodded. "I've got a work order with detailed instructions."

"Let me know if you need anything from me," CJ said. "I'll be out here, manning my desk." She left the door open only a crack. Enough that Cole could hear her, but not enough that anyone could see him sitting at Carpenter's desk, downloading data onto a portable hard drive.

CJ sat at her desk, facing the door to the hallway, her nerves on edge, fully expecting guards to come storming in looking for her with her fake clearance and identifying her as the person tapping into a computer hard drive. They'd haul her and Cole off and send them somewhere to be interrogated. Maybe even Guantanamo Bay to perform a little waterboarding on them to get what little information they could out of them.

Though she didn't care much what happened to her, she didn't want to see Cole thrown in jail for trying to help her find the Director of Trinity and put a stop to its form of terrorism.

A few minutes crawled by. CJ tapped her fingernails on the desktop, wondering how long it would take to make a complete backup of a desktop computer's hard drive.

She had just risen to go check on Cole's progress when a dark-haired young woman with a smooth, white complexion and coal-colored eyes entered the doorway to the hall and smiled. "I heard we had a replacement for Millicent." She entered, holding out her hand. "I'm Katie Wang, I work with the director for Europe and Russia."

CJ shook the woman's hand, trying to think of some way to get her out of there as soon as possible. "I'm Charlotte Jones. I'm just temporary staffing, filling in for Dr. Saunders. Is there something I could help you with?"

"I just wanted to let you know that I was working with Millicent on a project involving some connections in Russia. Mr. Carpenter knows about it. If he asks you to pick up the ball and run with it, you can call me. I can fill you in."

"Thank you. I'll be sure to do that. You're in the directory?" CJ asked.

"I am. Anything you might need, feel free to call." Katie headed for the door. "We were all sorry to hear about what happened to Millicent.

I visited her in the hospital. She's home now recovering."

"I'm glad to know that. I'm sure she will be missed while she's out."

"At least HR got it right on sending a replacement." Katie wiggled her fingers. "See ya around. And good luck."

As soon as Katie Wang left the office, CJ pushed through the door into Carpenter's office. "How's it going? Need help moving furniture?"

"Not yet. I need another five minutes to complete this download." Cole nodded at the computer and the flash drive sticking out of the front.

"Carpenter is supposed to be out of his office all morning," CJ said. "I don't expect him back anytime soon."

"Convenient. Maybe you can help me. The work order shows he wants the credenza moved to the west wall."

"Let me check out front and then I'll be back." CJ dashed out into the front office. Since it was empty, she turned back to the Homeland Security Advisor's office. She was just about to push through the door again when she heard voices in the hallway. One in particular was very familiar and had her heart racing.

She ducked her head into the inner office. "Got a problem. I hear Carpenter heading this direction."

"I can't stop the download now, or I'll have to start all over again." Cole glanced at the monitor and shook his head. "I need another three minutes."

"I'll do the best I can," CJ said and ran to her desk in time to take her seat.

Chris Carpenter entered the area with another man CJ didn't recognize at his side. "I have that file on my desk. I'll only be a second."

CJ stood and blocked Carpenter's path. "Oh, good. I'm glad you came back. I'm stuck and need a little guidance on one of the items on your list."

The Advisor tried to step around her. "I don't have time to help. Ask someone in one of the other offices to assist. I need to grab a file and go."

"Sir, the technical services guy just got here." CJ went to Carpenter's office door and stopped, her fingers curling around the handle. "Did you want to give him any directions on how you want your office arranged? He's ready to begin but had some questions."

"It's about time tech services got here. I put that work order in over a month ago. Yes, I'll speak with him." He turned to the man waiting in the doorway to the hall and held up a finger. "Give me two minutes."

The man nodded.

CJ prayed Cole had managed to cover the flash drive as she pushed the door open. "Mr. Carpenter is here. You can ask him what you wanted to know now."

Cole stood by the blank wall, away from the computer and monitor. "Is this the wall you wanted the credenza on?"

Carpenter nodded. "It is."

"Did you want it centered or offset to the right or left?"

CJ walked around the desk and stared at the wall with her head tilted to one side. "Centered would look good," she said. She shot a glance at the computer monitor. Cole had turned it off. Though the computer hummed as the files and data downloaded to the flash drive, having the monitor off made it appear as if the computer was powered down or in hibernation mode.

"Yes, centered," Carpenter was saying. "And I want my desk positioned in front of it with a gap between them similar to the one I have now. I need room to get in and out of my chair."

"Got it," Cole said.

The computer humming stopped and the light on the flash drive blinked off. The download had completed, CJ noted, just as Carpenter turned toward the desk.

"One other thing, Mr. Carpenter," Cole said, directing the man's attention back to him. "Did you want me to wire your computer for two monitors while I'm at it?"

"I don't need two monitors. One is more than enough."

While Carpenter's back was turned, CJ reached out, snatched the small device from the USB port and slipped it into her pocket.

Carpenter crossed to his desk, grabbed a file folder sitting on the corner and turned toward the exit. "Just move the desk and credenza. Everything else needs to stay the same. I'll be back later this afternoon."

Carpenter left the room and joined the other man waiting in the outer office, holding up the file. "Got it."

CJ followed them to the door. "If you need anything, Mr. Carpenter, all you have to do is call," she said.

He ignored her and disappeared down the hallway.

Once the Homeland Security Advisor was out of sight, CJ returned to the inner office. "Need help moving that furniture?"

He nodded. "Let's do it."

It took longer than expected to empty out drawers and shelves before they could move the furniture and reconnect the computer to an electrical outlet and ethernet port across the room. When they were done, it was noon.

"I'm going to get some lunch," CJ said. "Care to join me?"

"Don't mind if I do." Cole gathered his tools into the bag Jonah had equipped him with and they left Carpenter's office and exited the West Wing.

As they walked toward the food trucks lining the street for the lunch hour, Cole asked, "Think they'll miss you when you don't return from lunch?"

"I left a note on Carpenter's email telling him that I had been called to fill a permanent position and appreciated his understanding of the change." CJ grinned. "Hopefully, he won't be looking for me, or asking HR about me."

Cole dug his phone out of his pocket and placed a call. "Jonah, Cole here. We're out of the West Wing." He paused, listening. "Good. Then we'll head to Carpenter's home next. Thanks for taking care of it." He ended the call and nodded at CJ. "Jonah's on it. He shows Charlotte Jones as having been terminated from the HR database as of today, with the reason that you found other employment."

"Good. So, we're off to visit Carpenter's home next?"

"We are. Roger has what we'll need staged in a van off F Street, three blocks down. Everything is in that van."

"Address?" she asked.

"In Foxhall Village. Not far from here."

"Then let's do this." She picked up the pace, eager to get to Carpenter's place with the hope they'd find something, anything, that would lead them to the head of Trinity.

"What if Carpenter isn't our connection?" CJ said.

"Then we would mark him off the list and keep looking. I have to believe that text to Tully has to lead somewhere."

"He said he didn't have his phone that day."

"He could have lied," Cole pointed out.

They paused at a crosswalk and waited for the walking-man signal to blink on.

CJ was careful to check both directions. After Dr. Millicent Saunders had been run down crossing just such a street, they couldn't be too careful.

They made it across the street and hurried down F Street. At the third block, a white van was pulling out of a parking garage. The lettering on the side read *Bug-B-Gone*. Roger Arnold was at the wheel, wearing a white coverall with a patch with the same Bug-B-Gone logo embroidered over the right breast.

The side door slid open and Mustang waved them in.

CJ stepped in first, followed by Cole.

As soon as they were inside and the door was closed, Arnold headed for Foxhall Village. Next stop was Carpenter's home. CJ hoped they struck information gold. They needed a break. John Halverson had spent years searching for the answers. It was time to lay Trinity to rest. Preferably in a graveyard.

Chapter Nine

Cole sat on the floor inside the van, shaking his head. "You're kidding, right?"

"It's the perfect cover, isn't it?" Mustang grinned across at him.

"Did you get it?" Jonah sat on a bench in front of a laptop and an array of three monitors, holding out his hand.

CJ handed Cole the flash drive.

Cole placed it into Jonah's open palm. "When did we get a communications van?"

Mustang's grin broadened. "Charlie and Jonah had it in the works. This is its maiden voyage. Check it out." He pulled a panel across, hiding Jonah and his computers from sight. On the panel were face masks, gloves and plastic jugs of bug spray like those used by exterminators. "There's another panel near the rear door just like this. Anyone who just happens to look inside would never suspect there was a man and a bank of computer equipment inside."

Mustang reopened the panel, exposing Jonah at work, plugging the flash drive into a USB port on his laptop.

"I'll be looking through the data you collected from Carpenter's work computer while you collect the same information from his home computer." Jonah didn't look up as his fingers flew across the keyboard and mouse pad. The monitors flashed data on the screens.

"In the meantime, we need to dress for the part." Mustang handed them each a white coverall with the exterminator logo patch. "This is how we're getting into Carpenter's house. They're due an annual termite inspection. We're just going to do it earlier than they expected."

CJ's brow furrowed. "What about Mrs. Carpenter or the help?"

"Mrs. Carpenter is scheduled to meet with her hairdresser this afternoon. She should be gone during the time we're conducting our termite inspection," Mustang said.

"What if she gets done early?" Cole asked.

"That's why we have our communications van," Jonah said. "You, CJ and Mustang will have two-way communications. If we see anyone coming home early, we'll notify you. Hopefully, in time to get out."

Cole frowned. "Hopefully?"

"The house should have at least a front and a back door and possibly one in the kitchen," Arnold said. "You should be able to get out of one of them if I notify you as soon as someone shows up."

"We should," Cole said. "At the very least, if Mrs. Carpenter returns early and catches us at it, we can say Mr. Carpenter authorized us to conduct the termite inspection."

"If it comes to that, I can jam her cell phone signal," Jonah said, "long enough for you two to get out."

Mustang slid his legs into a white jumpsuit and pulled it up over his body. "I'll be on the outside, keeping watch, as well as to make sure we don't miss anyone sneaking in from other directions."

"Where are Gus and Jack?"

"Jack's still in the West Wing with Anne," Mustang said. "We can't be certain Trinity has been eradicated from the White House. Gus is following up on a tip from the dark web. A dog trainer in the Virginia countryside thinks there's a terrorist training camp in the hills near him. We sent Gus out with a drone to check it out."

CJ's eyes widened. "I remember being in the hills when I was in training with Trinity."

"Think you could find it again?" Cole asked.

She shook her head. "Operatives are taken out

of the camp blindfolded. Only the trainers know how to get in and get out."

"What about flying over?" Mustang zipped up his coverall.

CJ's eyes narrowed. "Maybe. I remember being in the woods, though. Even the buildings were surrounded by trees and hidden beneath the canopy."

"I look forward to Gus's report when he gets back," Cole said.

"Me, too." CJ glanced at the coverall in her hands. "I'll need to lose the skirt if I want to get into this," she said.

"I brought your backpack from the car," Arnold said from the driver's seat. "It's in the corner storage bin."

"Perfect." CJ found her backpack, tucked away the glasses and heels, and dug out a pair of gray leggings. Without hesitation, she slipped them up under her skirt. Once she had them on, she unzipped and stepped out of the skirt, folding it neatly before stuffing it into her backpack.

The coveralls went on over her leggings and shirt. She pulled them up over her hips and torso and slid her arms into the sleeves. The coveralls were two sizes too big, but she zipped them anyway and rolled up the sleeves. She shed the wig and rearranged her ponytail before fitting one of the green Bug-B-Gone hats over her head. Once more, she dug in her backpack and unearthed a pair of running shoes.

Cole marveled at how the woman could change her appearance so quickly and completely. No one would think she was the same person who'd stepped into the van wearing the black skirt and white blouse. She looked like a guy. A smallish guy with feminine facial features. "Do you carry everything in your backpack?" he asked.

"Everything I think I might need for a quick change in disguise." She lifted her chin. "It's kept me alive for the past year."

Cole held up his hands. "I'm not judging. I'm impressed."

"We'll be there in two minutes," Arnold called out.

Cole hurriedly dragged his coveralls on over his suit trousers. Removing his jacket and tie, he tugged the coverall sleeves on and zipped the white fabric over his shirt. He pulled on a cap and tugged paper booties over his dress shoes.

Jonah turned to Cole. "The Carpenters have an alarm system on their house. I've hacked into the company that services it and disarmed it for now."

"Good to know. Did you hack into their locks?" Cole gave Jonah a crooked grin. "Lock picking wasn't one of the skills we learned as Marine Force Recon."

"I've got that," CJ said.

Mustang shook his head, his lips twisting. "Trinity life lesson?"

CJ nodded. "From a young age."

"Need any tools?" Jonah asked.

One more time, CJ dug in the backpack and pulled out a thin file. "No. I've got it covered."

"Good," Arnold said. "Because we're here." He pulled to a stop on the side of the road between two large homes. He nodded at one. "Carpenters live in the gray brick house."

"Guess that's our cue," Cole said.

Jonah handed each of them an earbud. "These are your radio headsets. Turn them on and leave them on so you can hear me if I need to warn you of someone coming."

Mustang, Cole and CJ tested their communications devices one by one. When they were satisfied they could hear and be heard, Mustang closed the panel, hiding Jonah.

Cole opened the van's side panel and stepped out.

CJ followed and Mustang brought up the rear, carrying a jug of bug spray.

"I'll go around to the left, you two take the right," Mustang said. He left them and started around the front of the house, squirting bug spray as he went.

CJ led the way around the other side of the house. The house had a detached garage with a covered walkway between it and the kitchen entrance. CJ stuck her file into the lock on the handle, jiggled it once and had the kitchen door open within seconds.

Cole let out a low whistle. "I'm impressed."

She shrugged. "Like I said, they taught us the skill at an early age."

Cole followed her into the house, closing the door behind them, locking it in case someone did enter while they were there and were alerted to the fact the door wasn't locked.

They made quick work of the ground level. It consisted of a formal dining room, chef's kitchen, and a formal living room sporting a baby grand piano. In the back of the house was a den with a couple of comfortable sofas and lounge chairs.

CJ met Cole in the hallway near the staircase.

"His office must be upstairs," Cole said.

"All clear out back," Mustang said into Cole's headset.

"All clear in front," Arnold echoed.

Cole led the way up the stairs where they found three spacious bedrooms, a bathroom in the hall and the master suite at the end. Off the side of the master suite was another room with a desk, file cabinet, computer and a wall full of bookshelves.

"I'll download," Cole said.

"I'll look through his files." CJ crossed to the

file cabinet. It was locked, but she opened it with no problem.

Cole clicked the mouse only to find the computer was password protected. "Any idea what password he might use?"

"Try his birth month and year." Jonah gave him the numbers.

Cole keyed them in. It didn't work. "Next?"

"His wife's birth month and year." Again, Jonah fed him the numbers.

Cole entered them and he made it past the first hurdle. "Bingo." He stuck the flash drive into the USB port and started the download. While the computer was copying the files to the portable drive, he searched through Carpenter's emails, social media and internet cookies.

Many of the links were to news, travel and government sites typically visited by officials. One of the travel sites contained information about Russia. Another link took him to the site for the Russian embassy. In particular, to one of the embassy staff members, Sergei Orlov.

Cole pulled out his cell phone and snapped a photo of the name to remember later. He took another photo of the internet browser history.

With four more minutes to kill while waiting for the download to complete, Cole clicked on one IP address after another. Halfway down the list, he hit on one that brought up an image of the

Trinity knot. The same symbol found on a ring John Halverson had in his collection. The same symbol that kept popping up in connection with the Trinity organization.

A gasp sounded from behind him. "That's the Trinity website."

He turned to find CJ standing behind him, a file in her hand, her face pale.

"They have a website? I would have thought they'd want to be a lot lower key."

"They use it to recruit young people to their organization."

Cole clicked on the link. It took him to a video of teenage boys and girls, wearing camouflage, learning combat techniques and how to fire military-grade weapons, including AR-15s and grenade launchers. "I thought they took children from foster care?"

"They do, but they also recruit teens who rebel against authority or are looking for a place to fit in."

The video went on to show the young people sitting around a campfire in the woods, laughing and smiling.

CJ snorted. "They had to have used stock videos for that shot. We never sat around a campfire laughing and smiling. If we weren't training for combat, we were studying languages and other subjects to help us fit in to just about any situation or country."

"We've got company," Arnold said into their earbuds. "Silver Mercedes just blew into the driveway. Female getting out. I assume it's Mrs. Carpenter, by her appearance. She was going so fast I didn't realize she was going to stop until she turned in."

"Can you two get out?" Mustang asked from his position outside the house.

"We're upstairs," Cole whispered. "We'll hide and wait until she leaves." He exited the Trinity video and checked the status of the download. They needed two more minutes. He left it running in the background and prayed Mrs. Carpenter didn't notice the flash drive in the USB port.

"If she doesn't leave soon, we'll come up with a diversion to lure her out," Arnold advised them.

The sound of a door opening downstairs echoed up to the office off the master bedroom.

CJ tipped her head toward a closet at one end of the little office.

Cole followed CJ through the door, closing it behind them almost all of the way, leaving a little gap to let in light and sound. The closet was barely big enough for one person to fit inside, much less two. It contained a stack of file boxes, shoe boxes and one umbrella. CJ had moved to the side as far as she could to allow Cole to get his entire body inside the confined space.

He reached for her hand and held it, squeezing gently. He liked how soft yet strong her fingers were against his.

Footsteps sounded on the staircase and then in the upper hallway, heading in their direction.

Cole peered through the sliver of a gap in the doorway at the woman who entered the bedroom in a hurry, a cell phone to her ear.

"He's not home," she was saying. "I know... I had to come back. I forgot to clear the browser history before I left earlier. I know... I know... it was stupid and careless. But I'm here now and deleting it as we speak. He's been at the office all day. He'll never see it." She sat at the desk and clicked on the keyboard, hitting the delete button several times until she was satisfied. "There. All the browsing history has been wiped clean. I'll be there in twenty minutes." She smiled. "I'll be there soon, my love."

She ended the call, stood and looked down at the computer.

Cole tensed.

Had she noticed the flash drive? Or had she brought up the screen showing how many minutes were left on the download?

Mrs. Carpenter ran her fingers through her hair, closed her eyes and tipped her head back.

Then she left the little office and hurried through the bedroom to the bathroom on the other side.

"What's happening?" CJ whispered against his ear.

"She's in the bathroom," Cole answered so softly only CJ could hear.

The sound of the toilet flushing and water running in the sink was followed by Mrs. Carpenter leaving the bathroom and heading into the walk-in closet.

"Mustang?" Cole whispered softly into the headset.

"I read you," Mustang responded.

"Put a GPS tracker on her car," Cole said. "Now."

"Roger," Mustang responded.

Mrs. Carpenter emerged from the closet wearing a soft gray dress and red high heels. She slipped her arms into a black trench coat and left the bedroom, descending the stairs much slower than she'd climbed them.

A moment later, Cole heard the sound of the kitchen door clicking shut.

"The missus has left the building," Mustang said into Cole's headset.

"Did you get the GPS tracker on her car?" Cole asked.

"Roger."

"Good. We'll be down as soon as her car leaves the street," Cole told him, pushing the closet door open. "Be ready to track her." After checking that he couldn't see the driveway through the window, he strode to the desk and checked the status of the download. It was complete. He removed the flash drive and slipped it into his pocket. Then Cole pulled CJ into his embrace and dropped a kiss onto her lips. "I've wanted to do that all day. And I'd kiss you longer—"

"—but we have to follow that duplicitous Mrs. Carpenter." CJ took his hand and led him down the stairs and out through the kitchen door.

Mustang was already in the van when CJ and Cole climbed in.

"Follow her," Cole told Arnold as he handed Jonah the flash drive. He also texted him the two images he'd taken of the IP address to the Trinity recruiting site and of the Carpenters' browser history. "It's apparent that one of the Carpenters has a connection to Trinity. Seems it could be Chris Carpenter, Mrs. Carpenter or the man she'd called *my love* on her cell phone. Or it could be all three."

"Hopefully, one of them will take us to their leader," Jonah commented, his back to the others, busily tapping the keys on his laptop.

Cole prayed they would. He was ready to take down Trinity and put an end to their reign of terror. Then he could get back to making love to CJ without worrying someone was waiting in the sidelines to put a bullet through her head.

CJ UNZIPPED THE coveralls and stripped out of them. She sat cross-legged on the floor of the van, staring at the tracking device Mustang held in his hand in the passenger seat, directing Arnold through traffic.

"They aren't going to get anywhere really fast in this snarl," Mustang commented, looking at the bumper-to-bumper stream of cars.

"Neither are we," Cole pointed out, leaning over the back of Mustang's seat. "Where does she appear to be headed?"

"She's headed east on Reservoir Road," Mustang said. "No, wait. She's turning north on Thirty-Seventh Street."

Arnold drove the van out of Foxhall Village onto Reservoir Road.

A few moments later, Mustang reported, "Now she's on Tunlaw Road."

CJ leaned forward, her brow furrowed. "Isn't that close to Embassy Row?"

"I found a lot of travel sites in their travel history," Cole mentioned. "Wanna make a guess as to where?"

"Russia," Jonah said from behind them. "Someone was searching for flights to Moscow."

"Do you think Mrs. Carpenter is cheating on her husband with a Russian?" CJ asked.

"She's stopped in front of the Russian consulate," Mustang said. "Even if she's not cheating on her husband, she's meeting someone close to the consulate."

"There's no crime in that," Cole noted.

"No," CJ said. "But there is crime in attacking the White House and kidnapping the vice president and a mid-level staffer."

"True, but just because Mrs. Carpenter is stopping close to the Russian consulate doesn't mean she's meeting someone from the consulate, or that she was involved in the attack on the White House," Cole said.

"But she could be," CJ insisted, peering out the front window of the van as if she could see as far ahead as the consulate.

"She's moving again," Mustang said. "Heading for New Mexico Avenue."

"We're not far behind now," Arnold commented.

When the Carpenter woman stopped in front of the consulate, they'd gained ground and were now less than a couple of blocks behind her.

Her pulse pounding, CJ watched through the window, searching for a silver Mercedes. Ahead, traffic came to a stop at a light. The car in front of them turned onto a side street, leaving two cars between them and the silver Mercedes.

"There she is," Cole said.

"And she has someone in the car with her," Mustang noted.

The light turned green and they made a left onto Nebraska Avenue and a left on Arizona.

"I think they're headed for Chain Bridge," CJ said.

The light changed to red before they reached Arizona Avenue. The vehicle in front of them stopped. Had they been first to the light, CJ was certain Arnold would have blown through it. Instead the gap between them and Mrs. Carpenter lengthened.

By the time the light changed and they were moving again, the silver Mercedes had crossed Chain Bridge and merged onto George Washington Memorial Parkway heading north.

"Can we move any faster?" CJ asked, leaning over Arnold's shoulder.

"Only as fast as the people in front of us. We can gain some ground when we hit the parkway," Roger said.

Once on the major highway, they picked up speed. Roger adeptly zigzagged through the traffic, gaining on the woman in the Mercedes. Once again, they had closed the distance between them. Soon, they could see the silver sedan moving in and out of the fast lane.

Roger kept two cars between theirs and Mrs. Carpenter's, following her close enough to keep up, but far enough not to alert her to their presence.

A black sedan whipped past, swerving dangerously close to the vehicles in front of them. When it moved up alongside the silver Mercedes, it turned sharply into the side of the smaller vehicle. The Mercedes swerved violently, crossed the lane of traffic to its right and ran off the road, hitting a ditch and rolling several times before coming to a stop upside down.

Traffic slowed and Roger was able to get to the side of the road.

As soon as the van stopped, Cole ripped open the sliding door and they jumped out.

Cole was first to reach the crashed vehicle. CJ was next.

Mustang, Jonah and Roger brought up the rear, his cell pressed to his ear, reporting the accident to the 9-1-1 dispatcher.

Cole dropped to one knee and peered into the vehicle. Lying upside down, the top of the car had caved in several inches. "Doesn't look good." He tried to open the door, but the damage kept the door from budging.

CJ squatted beside Cole and looked in through the window.

Mrs. Carpenter lay crumpled against the ceiling. The man who'd been in the passenger seat lay across her, blood soaking his forehead. No airbags had deployed, making their injuries worse.

Neither moved.

"Let me in there," Arnold said.

Cole and CJ moved aside. Roger placed a tool against the window and the window glass exploded, creating a hole the size of his fist. Using the other end of the tool, he scraped the glass away from the frame.

Cole leaned in and touched two fingers to the base of the neck of the man lying over Mrs. Carpenter. He shook his head. "Not getting a pulse." He tried to get to Mrs. Carpenter's throat but couldn't with the man on top of her. "I can't get to the woman," he said.

Cole grabbed the man's arm and pulled. The dead weight and the angle didn't make it easy. "Help me get him out."

An acrid scent stung CJ's nose. "I smell gasoline." Smoke rose from the engine. "Need to get them out now!" She reached in, grabbed the man's other arm, braced her feet on the side of the vehicle and pulled with all her might.

With Cole pulling as well, they inched the man's body past the steering wheel and toward the window.

When Mustang could get close enough, he gripped the man's arm and added his weight to the tug-of-war.

The man broke free of whatever was holding him in and slid all the way out. "Check for identification," Cole called out and turned back to the upside-down vehicle.

CJ reached in, searching for Mrs. Carpenter's arm. A bloody hand grabbed her wrist.

She stared into the woman's open eyes through the blood staining her face. She tipped her head back to look into CJ's gaze. "Help me," she whispered, her words gurgling.

CJ held on to the woman's hand and pulled.

Cole reached in and hooked his hands beneath her shoulders and slid her the rest of the way out.

The woman kept a death grip on CJ's hand as Cole lifted her and carried her away from the vehicle.

Smoke turned to flame as the leaking gasoline caught and burned.

Cole, Mustang, Roger, Jonah and CJ ran up the embankment, putting as much distance as they could between them and the burning Mercedes.

No sooner had they reached the top of the embankment, the fire reached the gasoline in the tank and erupted in a blast that sent them to their knees.

Cole laid Mrs. Carpenter on the ground, covering her body with his as the ash rained down on them.

Sirens wailed in the distance, moving closer. Traffic had slowed and backed up with rubberneckers eager to see what was happening.

The hand on CJ's wrist slackened and the fingers released her.

CJ stared down into Mrs. Carpenter's eyes. "What do you know about Trinity?" she asked.

The woman gave a slight shake of her head. "They…did…this."

"We don't doubt that. We need to know who their leader is," CJ said, leaning closer. "Tell us."

Mrs. Carpenter shook her head. "Never."

"You'd let him kill you, rather than tell us who it is?" Cole leaned over the woman. "Trinity has to be stopped."

"Not until it's done."

"Until what's done?" CJ asked, tempted to shake the woman until she got answers.

"Soooonnn." Lydia Carpenter inhaled a shallow breath. Then all the air left her lungs, as if on a sigh, and she breathed no more.

Cole cursed.

CJ checked the woman for injuries. Other than a gash on her forehead, she appeared to be fine. She hadn't been wearing her seat belt. Nor had the man who'd been with her. Internal injuries could have taken their toll. CJ couldn't let it go. She pressed the heel of her palm against the woman's chest and pumped several times.

Cole felt for a pulse and shook his head.

"She knows something," CJ said through gritted teeth as she knelt beside the woman and performed CPR, continuing until the EMTs arrived and took over.

They worked on Mrs. Carpenter even as they loaded her into the ambulance and drove away.

CJ wiped the blood from her hands down the sides of her leggings, her heart pinching hard in her chest. "She knew something," she repeated.

Cole slipped an arm around her middle and pulled her against him. "We'll follow that lead. Everyone she's been in contact with. We'll look at her phone records and check into her passenger's identity. Surely he had connections to Trinity, as well."

CJ nodded. She'd seen her share of dead bodies, but this person had been the closest to being able to give her the answers they so desperately needed. So damned close.

"Come on. We need to get back to Charlie's estate and fire up the main computers." Cole turned her toward the exterminator van. "We have work to do."

Chapter Ten

It took Arnold over an hour to get them back to Charlie's. As always in the DC area, roads resembled a parking lot.

While Jonah worked on picking through the data on the flash drives as they sat in traffic, Cole could do nothing without a computer of his own. They'd tracked down the leads they'd had. Now they had to dig deeper into these new ones.

"Do you think Chris Carpenter is involved?" CJ asked.

Cole shook his head. Based on what they knew so far, he doubted it. "He could have been telling the truth when he said he'd left his phone at home the day of the attack. Likely his wife sent the text to Tully."

"Someone should question him about his wife's connection with the Russian."

"Sergei Orlov," Jonah called out from his position at the laptop inside the van. "I got a look at his wallet prior to the EMTs arriving to collect the bodies."

"What have you got on him?" Mustang asked.

"He works at the Russian consulate as some kind of staffer," Jonah reported. "He's been in the States for over a year and has no criminal record."

Cole pulled out his cell phone and dialed the estate.

"Halverson Estate, Grace speaking."

"Grace. How's Declan?"

"He's here, refusing to take pain meds and grouchy as a grizzly bear with a sore paw. But he's alive. Want to talk to him?"

"Yes, please," Cole said. "Put him on."

"Cole. You gotta get me outta here. These women are going to smother me to death. I'm fine. I can go back to work."

"The doctor said two weeks without lifting anything heavier than your hand," Grace said in the background. "That means lifting a gun is out of the question."

"My gun is not that heavy," Declan grumbled. "Forget about me, Cole. What's happening?"

Cole brought him up to date on the visit to Carpenter's office and home. When he got to the part about the phone conversation between Lydia Carpenter and her lover, Declan interrupted.

"She was having an affair with a Russian?" Declan whistled. "Affairs in Washington are practically public knowledge. No one in DC ever gets away with anything juicy like that for long."

"Apparently, Mrs. Carpenter was."

"And you caught her," Declan said.

Cole went on to explain about the accident and the Russian's death and Mrs. Carpenter's words.

"By the way," Jonah said. "I hacked into the hospital records. They called it. Lydia Carpenter is officially deceased."

"Chris Carpenter should be on his way to the hospital, if he's not there already."

"I'll have Snow intercept Carpenter to see what he can find out about the missus and her lover," Declan said.

"We're headed back to the estate," Cole said. "Unless you can think of anywhere else we should go at this point."

"No," Declan said. "We need to put our heads together and think about our next steps before we take them."

"You don't need to do anything but take your pain meds and sleep," Grace said in the background.

"I'm beginning to regret the relationship portion of this gig. I liked it better when I made my own decisions about what my body could or couldn't take," Declan grumbled.

"You can't let your wound get infected," Cole

said. "Let yourself heal before you jump back into the thick of things."

"Great," Declan muttered. "All I need is one more person telling me how to recuperate."

"Like I said," Grace murmured in the distance, "grizzly bear cranky."

"You would be, too, if you were stuck with a bullet wound when your team is out risking their lives." Declan cursed. "See you guys when you get here. If I haven't died of boredom by then."

Forty-five minutes later, the van pulled through the gate of the Halverson estate and rolled to a stop in front of the mansion.

Declan, Jack and Grace met them at the top of the steps.

Declan held a hand over his middle, his forehead creased.

"You didn't have to come out to greet us," Mustang said.

"I needed some air," Declan said and turned, wincing. "Hurts like the dickens."

"It wouldn't hurt as bad if you'd take the pain medication the doctor prescribed," Grace reminded him, slipping her arm around his back.

Declan draped his arm over her shoulder and leaned into her. "I can't take those drugs. They make my brain fuzzy. I get the feeling we're on the cusp of something big. I need a clear mind to think through what's going on."

"Fine. But at least find a place to stretch out," Grace said softly. "I don't like it when you're in pain."

He kissed her cheek. "I'll be okay. You're not getting rid of me anytime soon."

"I hope not. I haven't had nearly enough time with you. I want more."

Declan laughed. "Even when I'm surly?"

She smiled up at him. "Even when you're surly." Then she rose up on her toes and pressed her lips to his in a light kiss. "If you'll follow us, I had the guys set up a lounge chair in the war room for Declan before Gus left."

Declan tipped his head toward Jack. "Snow checked with the hospital to track down Chris Carpenter. He never showed up. Mack's in the war room, going through the video images that Gus is transmitting via the drone."

Carrying his laptop and the two flash drives, Jonah ducked past the people standing at the entrance and hurried inside.

Declan watched as he disappeared into the study. "Has Jonah found anything useful from Carpenter's computers?"

"The URLs and IP addresses were the most interesting items we found on the Carpenters' home computer. Jonah's digging into Sergei Orlov's background. All we know so far is that he works at the Russian consulate."

They entered John Halverson's study and descended the stairs into the basement war room.

Jonah was already hard at work, searching the internet for clues and answers.

Mack sat at the other computer with a screen showing the tops of trees, roofs on houses and barns and an occasional pond.

"Anything?" Declan asked.

"Nothing yet," Mack responded. He glanced up briefly. "Heard you guys had an interesting day."

Cole snorted. "To say the least."

Mack grinned. "Didn't expect to uncover a politician's wife cheating with a Russian, did you?"

"No, we didn't," CJ said.

"At least it was interesting. I've been staring at this screen for over an hour and haven't found anything nearly as cool as what you guys did." He returned his attention to the monitor.

CJ crossed the room to look over Mack's shoulder. "The compound where I was trained was pretty much buried in foliage. It won't be that easy to spot from the ground or air. Want help?"

"Sure." Mack pulled another chair close to where he was sitting. "Between you, me and Gus, three sets of eyes ought to be able to find something." He pointed to the monitor. "The dog trainer who gave us the info has a training facility here." He pointed to a spot on the screen where trees had been cleared and all that remained was a green grassy area. "He said the facility is off a road a couple of miles from his place to the northwest."

"What made him go that way?" CJ asked.

"He lost a dog he'd been boarding and went looking with a tracking dog. He found the animal, but also heard a lot of gunfire. When he got up close, he noticed the facility was surrounded by chain-link fence topped with razor-sharp concertina wire."

"Gunfire could be from a couple of guys out target practicing with pop cans, getting ready for deer season," Cole said, coming to stand behind CJ.

"Yeah, but they weren't firing single rounds, they were firing semiautomatic and automatic weapons, from what the dog trainer said." Mack pointed to the northwest of the dog facility. "The trees are dense here, and there are more hills to hide in."

CJ leaned closer to the monitor, looking for anything that didn't fit in, like the straight edge of a roofline or vehicle. The more she looked, the more the green leaves of the trees blended together. Until she came to a dark, rusty line in the middle of a canopy of trees. "There," she said, pointing to the line. "Is that a corrugated tin roof?"

Mack zoomed in on the image, blowing it up to twice the size on the screen. "Looks like it."

Following the line of the roof, CJ found another shape that wasn't natural for a forest, a gray, curved bowl. "Satellite dish?" she said, her brow dipping.

Mack nodded and pointed to another straight line. "That appears to be another building tucked beneath the trees."

Soon, they'd identified several potential buildings.

Mack picked up a satellite phone and called Gus. "Any way you can get closer to these coordinates?" He gave Gus the numbers and waited.

When Gus finally spoke again, Mack's brow furrowed. "Got it. So, it's like the dog trainer said. Did you hear any sounds of gunfire?"

CJ could hear Gus talking, but couldn't make out the words.

Mack's gaze met Cole's. "No sounds. Maybe they've moved from that site." He paused while Gus spoke. "You did? I'd say it's time to go in and investigate, boots on the ground."

"We're in." Cole glanced across at CJ.

She nodded, her pulse pounding hard against her eardrums. Heading back to where it all began seemed insane, but necessary. They might find the leader of Trinity there, supervising the training of even more Trinity agents. A bunch of babies being led into a life of violence.

If she had any way of getting them out, she would. "Let's go."

"We'll get back with you when we have a plan and timeline," Mack assured Gus. "Stay low and don't get caught." Mack ended the call and turned to Cole. "We need communications equipment, bulletproof vests, weapons and some smoke grenades."

"Are we going in prepared to shoot kids?" Cole asked.

"No, but we're going in prepared to defend our lives," Mack said.

"Who's going where?" Charlie's voice sounded from the top of the stairs.

All gazes turned to the woman who funded their little band of brothers.

Charlie Halverson looked like a million bucks. Dressed in a long, silver-beaded, satin-and-lace gown, she looked like royalty as she descended the stairs one step at time.

She glanced around the room. "I thought everyone was headed in for the night." Her gaze settled on Declan. "And that Declan was going to get some rest."

"We think we may have found one of Trinity's training camps," Mack said.

Charlie moved forward, her eyes widening.

"Do I need to stay home tonight and help monitor activities?" she asked.

Declan frowned. "You're going out?"

"I had an invitation to a special event where the president is scheduled to speak," Charlie said.

"Charlie, you have to go to the event," Grace said. "That's more important."

"If anything, we could wait to move in on the training camp until another day," Declan said. "If they're still using the camp, I doubt they'd get out of there sooner."

"No." Charlie held up a hand. "You do what you have to do."

"But we can't leave you unprotected. Someone needs to go with you to the event," Declan insisted. He tried to rise to his feet, but he couldn't bend over enough to lean forward. Instead he sat back in the lounge chair and winced. "I'll go with Charlie to the event. As soon as someone helps me out of this chair."

"You're not going anywhere," Grace said. "I'll go with Charlie."

Declan frowned. "You aren't trained in hand-to-hand combat and they won't let you in if you carry a gun." He glanced around the room, his gaze landing on Roger Arnold, who was just descending the stairs carrying a tray filled with a pitcher and glasses. "Arnold and I will go to the event with Charlie. The rest of the team will check out the compound. If you determine the place is a Trinity training camp, you are not to engage. You will fall back and call in the FBI, national guard and whoever else we need to round up all of the operatives."

"And don't forget the children," CJ said. "They'll need special handling. They'll be well on their way to being brainwashed."

"If you're going with Charlie, I am, too," Grace said.

"I can't get everyone in. I can only bring a plus one," Charlie said. "Roger will be my plus one." She turned to him with a frown. "We'll need to have you fitted immediately with a tuxedo."

"I have one, ma'am," Arnold said.

Her eyes widened. "You do?" Then her brow dipped. "Why did I not know this about you, Roger?"

He straightened to his full height, shoulders back and chest puffed out like the military man he'd once been. "Because you never asked."

Charlie smiled. "Roger, you take such good care of me."

"Yes, ma'am," he said.

"You'll have to stop calling me 'ma'am' if you're coming with me tonight."

"Yes, Charlotte," he said, his voice softer.

CJ hid a smile. She might not be an expert in the ways of the heart, but she could swear there was something there in Roger's eyes. A flash of desire or longing? Or was CJ projecting her own feelings for Cole into those around her?

CJ sighed. Until they resolved the Trinity issue, she couldn't have any kind of long-term relationship with anyone without putting them at risk. As much as she loved being around Cole, she'd have to cut the ties forming and leave. A heaviness settled on her chest. She hadn't felt that kind of weight since she'd lost her parents.

Mack had risen and gone to the cabinets against the wall. One by one, he pulled out weapons, grenades, bulletproof vests and communications devices.

Jonah helped him organize and store them in a couple of large duffel bags.

"I'll bring the SUV around to the front of the house," Roger Arnold offered and left the room, climbing the stairs, his limp barely noticeable.

Charlie's gaze followed him up the stairs, the corners of her mouth curling upward. "Arnold—Roger," she corrected, "never ceases to surprise me. And we've known each other since I met my husband. He was in the SAS when the three of us met in a bar in London." She smiled. "At first I was more attracted to Roger than John." She pressed her hands to her chest. "There's something about a man in uniform that makes a girl's heart flutter." She drew in a deep breath and let it out. "Alas, Roger deployed to some godforsaken place in Africa and John swept me off my feet." She turned to CJ, her eyes misty with unshed tears. "I loved John with all my heart."

CJ nodded, not knowing what to say to the woman. She had no experience with love. Her gaze went to Cole as he loaded rounds into magazines to be used in the weapons they would take. What would it be like to be loved by a man the way John had loved Charlie?

Dragging her gaze away, CJ squared her shoulders, grabbed a box of bullets and fit them into still more magazines. Though they weren't going in with the intention of starting a fight, they might be forced to defend themselves and the children who'd been recruited by Trinity.

"The most important thing we have to be aware of is Trinity's leader," Cole said. "If he's at the compound, we can't let him escape."

"True," Declan agreed. "If it comes to a choice between losing him or engaging with the enemy… engage the enemy to save the children."

CJ loaded more magazines. If they had to engage the enemy, they might be shooting teenagers and children. She prayed it didn't come to that.

For the first time in a year, she had a chance at finding and neutralizing the leader of an organization that had ruined the lives of many children, including her life. They had to make this opportunity count. She didn't know if she had the strength to continue a life of looking over her shoulder.

CJ wanted more. She wanted love and maybe a family of her own.

She'd never even considered children as part of her future, never saw them fitting in, so she'd not given the possibility any thought. Now, though, she realized there were many things she wanted that she'd simply refused to allow herself to contemplate as a member of Trinity and then as an escapee from their evil grasp.

But, yes, she wanted children, damn it. After all she'd been through, all she'd been trained to be, she hadn't considered herself fit to be a mother. Hell, she'd thought she wasn't fit to be the wife of a good man.

But now—now she had dreams.

Chapter Eleven

Cole rode in the middle row of seats of the SUV. Mack drove, Jack claimed shotgun and CJ sat beside Cole. Mustang sat in the backseat as they drove through late-evening DC traffic to the Leesburg airport outside of the city. Charlie's connections had arranged for a helicopter to ferry them to a location close enough to the compound that they could set down in a field and hike in from there. Gus, who would meet them on the fenced perimeter, would wait to move in until they were all there.

The helicopter was a model used for sightseeing. The pilot was a former army helicopter aviator. He didn't ask questions about the gear they brought on board in two large duffel bags. All he needed was the weights to balance the load and they were off, heading west farther into Virginia.

Where it had taken forty minutes for them to get from Charlie's estate to Leesburg Executive

Airport, it took less than thirty minutes for them to fly the distance from the airport to the landing site in the Virginia countryside.

Cole stared down at the traffic on the highway at a standstill in the evening rush hour and said a prayer of thanks for Charlie and her connections. It had taken Gus over an hour and a half to drive the same distance during the middle of the day, not at rush hour.

The pilot put down in the dog handler's field after Jonah had called ahead to get permission. The helicopter and pilot would remain in the field until one of the team released him to leave. If someone ended up getting hurt, they might have to airlift him out to get medical attention—quicker than waiting for an ambulance.

Cole hoped that didn't happen, but it was nice to know they had the helicopter as backup if they needed a quick getaway.

By the time they landed, the sun had just dropped below the horizon, casting the land into the gray shadow of dusk. They could see, but night would consume them quickly. The sooner they moved out, the better. Their night vision would adjust as the light faded.

Cole grabbed one of the bags and Mack took the other. They divided what was in them among the five members of the team, carrying an extra rifle for Gus who'd gone out with the drone and a handgun. Each person plugged the radio communications earbuds in their ears and buckled into bulletproof vests.

"How do we find Gus?" CJ asked.

"He's got the drone and it's wired with a GPS tracker." Mack held up a tracking device. "I have him, as long as he's still with the drone."

As they took off through the woods, Cole dropped back behind Mack and Jack. Mustang brought up the rear.

Cole reached for CJ's hand and held it as long as he could without tripping over branches and underbrush. Eventually, he was forced to let go. The darkness made it difficult to see what they were stepping on and into.

He wanted to ask her if she was all right, but the others would hear anything he had to say since they were all connected with the earbuds. He had to be satisfied that she was near him. Cole wasn't sure it was a good idea for her to go back into the compound if it was the one where she'd trained. Being back was sure to ignite a firestorm of memories that could end up derailing her concentration.

By the time they reached Gus, darkness had settled in and the stars had come out. A few clouds scudded across the sky, blocking out some of the light, but they could see well enough by moonlight to move through the forest without use of flashlights.

They found Gus seated beneath a tree, the drone on the ground beside him. When he saw them coming, he rose to his feet. "I did what I could to recon the area, but without wire cutters, I couldn't get past the fence without digging under."

"What did you find?" Cole asked.

"First, I checked, and this facility is not owned or operated by any federal or local authorities. It's private. The front gate has two sentries, each armed with AR-15 rifles. There's a guard at the rear of the compound inside the fence and one on each side. All are armed. I couldn't tell if the fence is designed to keep people out or in."

"Both," CJ answered.

Cole dug into his pocket, pulled out a pair of wire cutters and held them up. "Point us in the right direction and we'll get this party started."

Gus led them down a ravine and up the other side, over a ridge and back down to a fence that rose up out of the forest floor, eight feet high. It was topped with two more feet of concertina wire.

"The guard is a couple hundred yards to the south," Gus whispered.

"Cutting the wire is likely to make noise," Cole warned.

"We'll have to be ready in case he comes to check it out," Gus said.

Mack turned south. "Gus and I will keep an eye out for movement."

"Mustang and I will take the opposite direction," Jack said, "in case our man on the back side of the compound comes snooping."

CJ stood guard on Cole while he snipped through the chain-link fence one link at a time. He was glad she had his back. Standing at the fence, he would be easy to spot should anyone come anywhere close on the other side.

When he had cut enough of the links that a person his size could fit through, he stopped. Slipping the wire cutters into his pocket, he held the flap of fence to the side for CJ to go through first.

"We're in," he said into his headset.

Mack and Gus returned to his location and ducked through.

"We took care of our guard. He won't be warning the others of our arrival."

Mustang and Jack showed up at that moment. "We took out our guy. He won't be a problem. And we circled around to the far side and knocked out the one over there."

"Which leaves the two on the gate," Gus said.

After everyone else made it through, Mack held the fence for Cole. When they were all on the other side, they moved out slowly, staying low and clinging to the shadows.

Gus and Mack led the way based on the information they'd gleaned from the images the drone had collected. Treading quietly, they eventually could see several long buildings with corrugated tin roofs and clapboard walls.

"Dormitories," CJ whispered. "This is where they brought us. The one on the right is for the younger kids. The one on the left is for the teenagers. It's all coming back to me. In the center is a two-story house. It's the headquarters building. It's where the instructors live and dole out punishment."

"Get down," Mack said into the headset. "Someone's coming."

Several men carrying five-gallon jugs rounded the corners of the dormitories, shaking the contents of the jugs up against the sides of the buildings.

The scent of gasoline filled the air.

"That's gasoline. They're soaking the walls," CJ said. "They're going to burn the dormitories." She leaped to her feet and started toward the long buildings.

Cole dived after CJ, tackled her to the ground and covered her body with his, praying the men with the gasoline jugs hadn't seen her.

"They'll kill them," she wheezed, barely able to breathe beneath the weight of the former marine on her back.

"We don't know if there are any people in those dorms," Cole whispered in her ear. "And we don't know if those men are armed."

Mack and Jack slipped through the trees, darting from shadow to shadow until they were close enough to the men slinging gasoline all over the buildings.

"They're armed," Mack said softly.

"I'll get the one on the right," Jack said.

"Better make it fast—someone just threw a match," Cole said.

"Let me up." CJ bucked beneath him. "We have to help them."

"I will as soon as you promise not to go off half-cocked."

"I promise," she said too quickly.

"They're armed, CJ. You can't help those kids if you're dead."

"I can handle them. Let me go."

Cole rolled off her. "Stick to the shadows and be careful." He didn't want to let her go, but he had to. She was a trained killer, and she'd find a way out of his grasp no matter what he did. Better to let her go and help her than to have her work without his knowledge. CJ could take care of herself.

As she took off toward the dormitories, he prayed that was the case.

HER HEART SLAMMED against her ribs as CJ ran toward the first building, the one that housed the youngest of the children.

When the man dropped the match, flames spread and rose up the walls like a dancing, heaving blanket, consuming the gasoline and eating into the wooden walls.

Mack, Gus, Mustang and Jack sneaked up on the two men swinging around the rear of the dormitory with their jugs of gasoline. The Defenders took the two men out without making a sound.

As smoke and flame rose, sounds came from inside the dorms. Sounds of children coughing and crying for help. The building had no windows. CJ remembered there being a back door and a front door. Since the guys with the gas hadn't made it all the way around the building, the back door was still clear of the fire. CJ ran to the back door.

Hands banged on the door from the inside and voices shouted and screamed there.

CJ's heart squeezed hard in her chest. She tried the doorknob, then realized there was a padlock on the outside, locked tight. The men had locked the children inside and planned on burning the building down and the kids with it. This would cause a stir and attention, something Trinity liked to avoid, but CJ guessed in this case they might want to send a warning to people like her who got out. Trinity was ruthless enough to kill dozens of kids just to let a traitor know they'd stop at nothing.

CJ used the handle of her pistol and slammed it against the padlock again and again. No matter how hard she hit it, it wouldn't break. Then she remembered the file she'd placed in her pocket. She pulled it out, her hands shaking, and almost dropped it on the ground. After two attempts, she had the lock opened and removed from the hasp. Then she tackled the lock on the doorknob, releasing it on the first attempt. Finally, she flung open the door. Children rushed out, wearing the T-shirts and underwear they'd gone to bed in. Smoke billowed out with the children.

Mustang, Cole and CJ ran into the smoky room, checking beds and beneath the bunks. When the building was clear, they ran out, coughing.

CJ's lungs burned and her eyes stung, but there was another dormitory full of people and the flames were burning hotter and brighter from that building.

Mack, Gus and Jack had moved on to take out three other men wielding jugs of gasoline. These three had come looking for their cohorts and found Declan's Defenders. They were in the midst of hand-to-hand combat when Mustang, CJ and Cole arrived on the scene from behind.

Cole took out the one closest to him and CJ side kicked the other, sending him flying into Jack's fist. CJ didn't wait around to watch the outcome. She ran to the second dorm. Like the first, it had been locked from the outside with a padlock. Using her file, she unlocked the padlock on her first attempt and then the doorknob lock. Teenagers spilled out as soon as the door opened.

The ones closest to the doors stumbled out of the smoke-filled room, coughing and hacking. Some helped others escape. Still others lay on the floor, having succumbed to the smoke.

While Gus, Mustang and Jack went after the men on the gate, Cole and Mack helped CJ get everyone out of the second dorm, some leaning on them for support, others having to be lugged out in a fireman's carry over broad shoulders.

When Cole went back into the dormitory for the last teen, CJ turned toward the main house where the trainers lived and held court. They'd been the judges, juries and hangmen of the compound, keeping order through threats of harsh sentences. If the leader of Trinity was anywhere around, he'd be inside the main house, packing his stuff to get out before the fire department arrived and found all the dead children.

Would he be here at all? Part of her thought a leader this cruel would enjoy seeing his sickening plans in action, might even take pleasure in seeing her suffer as she witnessed the tragedy unfolding.

Anger burned inside CJ hotter than the actual fire as she ran toward the house. An SUV stood outside, the engine running and the headlights shining. Several men were inside the vehicle. The driver's door hung open and no one sat in the driver's seat. A smaller SUV stood in front of the larger one, also running but unoccupied.

A man came out of the house, got into the larger vehicle and started to drive around the one in front of it.

CJ couldn't let them get away. While running toward the vehicle, she pulled out her handgun, aimed for the tires and fired off one round after another. She hit the right front and rear tires. Windows lowered and guns poked out of them.

CJ dived to the ground and rolled behind the rusted-out hull of the abandoned 1957 Ford Fairlane that had been in the courtyard of the compound for as long as she could remember.

Bullets slammed into the metal and kicked up dust around her. She edged toward the opposite end of the massive pile of junk metal and fired several more rounds into the windows of the SUV. The driver swerved and hit the vehicle that had been parked in front of it, sending it sliding up against the front porch railing of the house.

A couple of the men dived out the doors onto the ground, rolled to their feet and started running.

CJ shot them in the legs. They fell to the ground, screaming and clutching at their wounds.

The flames from the burning dormitories lit

the yard, making it nearly impossible for her to run across to the big house without being seen.

Taking a deep breath, she left the comparative safety of the Fairlane and sprinted across the yard, heading for the house. She zigzagged, making it harder for potential shooters to get a bead on her.

Shots rang out, kicking up dust beside her.

She didn't slow until she reached the porch. Taking the steps two at a time, she dived through the door into the front foyer, rolled to the side and came up on her feet, her Glock in her hand.

"Stop right there," a voice said. A man stood before her with a handful of documents, fire burning one corner of them, and a pistol in his other hand, aimed at her chest.

With her heart pounding against her ribs, CJ stared down the barrel of the pistol and then looked up into the face of a man she recognized. Not from her time spent in training, but from her short time in the West Wing of the White House. "Chris Carpenter," she said aloud.

He gave a slight nod and tossed the papers onto the floor among a larger pile of documents and folders. The flames spread, gobbling up more paper, sending a bright flame climbing into the air.

"It's about time you came back to the fold, CJ." Carpenter shook his head. He brought his free hand up to stabilize the one holding the pistol. "I didn't recognize you when you took Dr. Saunders's position, I wasn't here when you went through training and I only had grainy photos to go by, so it didn't come to me right away. But once I learned you'd been in my house, I compared videos of the woman in my office with the one in the exterminator's outfit and realized my mistake. We taught you well."

"I'm not here for compliments, nor am I here to rejoin Trinity," CJ said. "I came to put a stop to Trinity and keep them from stealing children and killing innocent people."

"Like you kept them from killing my wife and Orlov, her lover?" Carpenter snorted. "I put out that kill order as well as the one that put a stop to John Halverson's snooping."

"You were responsible for John Halverson's death?" Her teeth ground together, her finger itching to pull the trigger.

"I had to. He knew too much."

"Bastard," she ground out.

"Maybe so. We had a job to do, and he was in the way. But no more. The wheels are turning, the plan is in place." He gave her a smile that looked more like a sneer. "And you're too late to stop it."

"Too late?" She frowned. "What do you mean?"

His lip curled. "The remaining recruits are being eliminated as we speak and, after tonight, our primary purpose will have been accomplished."

CJ lifted her chin, her eyes narrowing. "And that is?"

"Assassination of the most prominent figure in US government. In doing so, we'll put our own man in position to effect change." Carpenter snorted. "It's finally happening. What we've been working toward for so long."

"The president? Trinity is going to assassinate POTUS?" CJ's heart slid to the pit of her belly and back up to pound against her ribs. "When? How?"

Carpenter's lips twisted. "Sooner than you think. And we'll finally be rid of the other half of the Halverson annoyance."

CJ shook her head. "Charlie Halverson?"

"We thought we'd done away with the trouble when the Director had me eliminate John, never expecting his widow to pick up the baton and run with it." His jaw tightened. "But that will all be behind us soon." He took his gaze off her for a brief glance at his watch. "Yes, soon. Now, I need to get out of here before the gasoline tanks explode. You're going to be my ticket past your bodyguards."

"What makes you think I won't shoot you first?" CJ held the gun steady, her finger resting on the trigger. She'd always been taught never to put her finger on the trigger unless she intended to shoot.

She intended to shoot.

"You don't have it in you to shoot. You proved that when you wouldn't shoot your target a year ago."

"I don't shoot defenseless pregnant women," she said. "You're neither a woman, defenseless nor pregnant."

His eyes narrowed. "I could pull the trigger first, but if you die, you won't have time to warn your friends of the impending explosion. If you come with me without a fight, I won't shoot you. You can tell your friends about the tank before it goes up, and be my ticket out. I'll take you back to the people you belong with. You'll be an asset to us, with all you've learned on your little…vacation away from Trinity. But you only have a few seconds to make up your mind. What's it going to be?"

CJ didn't hesitate. She pulled the trigger, then dived to the side.

The sound of gunfire echoed in her ears and a sharp pain ripped through her shoulder as she hit the wooden floor hard, rolled and came up, her Glock pointed at the man still standing. He dropped the gun from his grip and stared across at her, his face pale. "Won't do you any good. This place will blow any minute… The president and Halverson—" he dropped to his knees, clutching at his chest, blood seeping through his fingers "—will be dead…and the Director—" Carpenter slid to his side and stared up at her "—will… be…in…charge." The corners of his lips curled upward. "You're too…late."

CJ turned, pain shooting through her at her sudden move. Warm liquid dripped down her left arm. She glanced at her jacket, surprised to see blood. It didn't matter. She didn't have time to deal with it—she had to warn the others.

As she stepped through the door, gunfire rang out. A bullet hit the door frame beside her. Splinters rained down on her.

CJ darted to the side and dropped to a prone position, flattening her body against the wooden slats of the porch. She searched the darkness for the shooter. A man stood beside the crippled SUV, aiming for her.

Before she could bring her weapon up to shoot the man, another shot rang out. Fully expecting to take the hit, CJ was surprised when she didn't feel the pain. The man by the SUV crumpled to the ground and lay still.

"CJ?" Cole's voice called out. "Are you all right?"

Her gaze swept the yard, landing on the man who'd captured her heart. He stood with his gun pointed at the SUV.

CJ's heart swelled. "I am," she said and rose to her feet. With no time to spare, CJ leaped off the porch and ran toward Cole. "We have to get everyone out of here. Now."

Mack, Mustang, Jack and Gus appeared, silhouetted against the blaze.

"The recruits are hiding in the woods," Gus said.

CJ shook her head, dread crushing her chest like an anvil. "We have to get them out of here. Now," she repeated. "They have explosives on the fuel storage barrels. It'll blow any minute."

"We'll round up the children and send them down the road," Mack said.

"Go!" CJ said.

The four men ran toward the woods behind the dormitory infernos.

"I'm afraid they'll be too late," CJ said to Cole. "I have to find the explosives." She started toward where she knew they kept the barrels of gasoline.

Cole's hand shot out and captured her arm. "You can't."

She shook loose. "I have to." Then she was running, her feet carrying her the fastest she could go toward the possibility of death. If she didn't get to the explosives before they went off, she'd be blown away and die a fiery death. But so, too, would Declan's Defenders and the children who'd been involuntarily recruited to become assassins.

She couldn't fail. Those kids deserved to be

children. Cole, Jack, Gus, Mustang and Mack descrved to live long, full lives.

If she died, no one would care, but they deserved to live.

Footsteps pounded on the ground behind her. Cole caught up with her and kept pace as she dodged between storage buildings to the back of the compound where the fuel was stored. Eight fifty-five-gallon barrels stood in a line. She didn't know which were empty and which were full. It didn't matter. What mattered was finding the explosives and disarming them before their world erupted into a fiery crescendo.

Cole started on one end, CJ on the other, as they examined the barrels, searching for the explosives. They met in the middle, both locating the wad of C-4 smashed up against a full barrel with a timing detonator pressed into the middle. The red digital numbers indicated thirty seconds until detonation.

CJ tried to pry the detonator loose from the C-4 plastic, but she couldn't get it to release.

Twenty-five seconds remained.

"Let me," Cole said. He dug his fingers into the C-4 and pulled as hard as he could, but he couldn't get the device out.

Ten seconds ticked by and still, they couldn't free the claylike plastic from the barrel or the detonator from the plastic.

Pulling her file out of her pocket, CJ rammed it beneath the C-4.

Nine seconds…eight…seven…

Cole found a stick and used it as well, prying the explosive free of the barrel with five seconds to spare.

He ran for the woods, cocked his arm and threw the device into the darkness. "Get down!" he yelled and dropped to the ground.

CJ dropped to her belly, closed her eyes and covered her ears.

An explosion rocked the ground beneath her. A loud cracking sound followed.

CJ looked up in time to see the dark shadow of a massive tree falling toward them.

"Cole! Run!" she cried. Instead of running away from the falling tree, she ran toward Cole.

He staggered to his feet and took off.

She caught up with him and they ran as fast as they could to get away from the massive tree falling toward the buildings of the compound and the barrels of gasoline.

As it fell, other trees slowed its descent, buying CJ and Cole enough time to get out of the way of the largest of the branches.

When it hit the ground, a branch full of leaves slammed into CJ's back, slapping her to the ground like a fly beneath a swatter.

Cole, a few steps away from her, staggered but regained his balance.

He parted the leaves and helped CJ to her feet.

They turned to survey the damage the giant tree had created. The acrid scent of fuel filled the air again.

"I smell gasoline," CJ said.

"The tree fell on the barrels. We have to go." Cole's quiet voice sent shivers down her spine.

CJ launched herself away from the tree, the barrels and the burning buildings that would soon catch the tree and the spilled gasoline on fire. They had only moments to spare.

As she ran, her ankle screamed with pain, until she was limping as fast as she could.

Cole slipped an arm around her waist and let her lean on him as they hurried away from impending disaster.

They were passing the main house when Cole veered toward the smaller SUV Chris Carpenter would have used as his getaway vehicle. It was still running with the driver's door still open.

Cole opened the passenger door. CJ dived in.

He rounded to the other side and slipped in behind the wheel. He'd just shifted into Drive when the barrels ignited, sending up balls of flames into the sky.

CJ could see the fiery reflection in the side mirror. "Go," she said. "We can't stop now. We have even bigger problems."

"What do you mean?" Cole asked.

Her fists clenched in her lap, a dull ache throbbing in her injured shoulder. "Trinity is planning a coup. They're targeting the president."

"When?"

"I assume tonight. Carpenter kept saying we were too late." She touched Cole's arm. "And they're taking Charlie out at the same time. They want the Director to take over as president."

"The only person who can do that is the VP. And if he's killed, then the speaker of the house."

"Where did Charlie say she was going tonight?" CJ asked.

Cole's fingers tightened on the steering wheel until his knuckles turned white. "She's at an event where the president is speaking."

"We have to get there." She leaned forward as they caught up with the children and teenagers walking down the middle of the road, heading for the highway.

They wore T-shirts and shorts, most barefoot, their eyes wide and scared. They looked like ghosts.

CJ's chest tightened. They would need years of counseling. What they'd gone through would have serious effects on them, much like PTSD for battle-weary soldiers.

She didn't have time to worry about them now. She had to gather the other men of Declan's Defenders and get back to the city before Carpenter's prediction came true and they were too late.

Chapter Twelve

Cole pulled up beside Mack, Mustang, Gus and Jack, each carrying a barefoot child piggyback. Sirens blared as fire trucks, law-enforcement vehicles and first responders pulled onto the dirt road leading to the compound, lights flashing like a parade with fast, colorful floats.

"We have to go," CJ said as the road became congested with people and vehicles. A smaller fire truck with paramedics on board was the first to reach them. The four Defenders handed over the children on their backs. Gus, Mustang and Jack got into the back of the SUV.

Mack gave the paramedic a brief explanation of what had happened and then backed away, slipping silently into the SUV.

Cole edged through the crowd of young people and headed for the highway, his pulse pounding, his hands holding the steering wheel so tightly he thought it would break. They couldn't get out of there fast enough.

Charlie had done so much for them. They couldn't let her down.

Jack was on his cell phone, desperately trying to contact Charlie, Roger or Declan. None of them was answering their cell phones. They would have made it to the downtown event center. Roger would be inside with Charlie. Declan would be with them, if Charlie arranged to have more than one escort. If not, he'd be nearby in case anything happened.

As soon as they reached the highway, Cole pressed the accelerator to the floor, sending the vehicle blasting toward the dog trainer's property and the waiting helicopter. Mack had called ahead to warn the pilot that they'd need to take off immediately.

The chopper was ready, the blades turning, when they pulled into the field.

Everyone bailed out of the SUV as soon as Cole pulled to a stop.

CJ and Cole hunkered low and ran toward the helicopter, climbing in.

Cole buckled his safety harness. When CJ fumbled with hers, he leaned over and pulled her harness over her shoulders. His hand brushed against warm, sticky liquid on her left shoulder. He leaned closer, staring hard at her in the limited lighting. "You're hurt."

She shrugged. "It's just a flesh wound." As if to prove it, she lifted her arm up and down. "See? I can still use it."

"We need to get you to a doctor."

"After we make sure Charlie and the president are okay, we'll have plenty of time to stick a bandage on this scratch," she said, her chin lifting in challenge. "Not any sooner."

Cole didn't like it. CJ was bleeding. She could have lost a lot of blood already.

As if reading his mind, she touched his arm. "If I'd lost a lot of blood, I wouldn't have been able to run to the helicopter. I was more worried about my ankle than my shoulder and it's fine. Both are fine. I'll survive. It would take a lot more to bring me down than a bullet or a 150-year-old tree." She cupped his cheek and smiled into his eyes. "I'm okay."

As soon as everyone was on board, Mack yelled into his flight headset, "Go! Go! Go!"

The chopper left the ground and rose into the air, turning in a tight circle toward the bright lights of the downtown area.

Because of the air restrictions around DC, the closest the pilot could land was at the Leesburg Leesburg Executive Airport. When the helicopter touched down, they dived out and ran for Charlie's SUV.

Mack drove, weaving in and out of traffic toward DC and the hotel hosting the event.

"We'll never get there in time," CJ said.

Traffic into the downtown area had thinned, allowing them to make good time, but they couldn't be certain they'd arrive before whatever Trinity had planned started.

Cole pulled out his cell. They couldn't wait another minute. "I'm calling in a bomb threat."

"We'll never get in after that," Mustang pointed out.

"No, but maybe they'll get out before Trinity attacks," Cole said.

They were five blocks away when police, fire trucks and ambulances raced past them toward the hotel. Traffic came to a halt.

"We have to get through before they barricade the streets," Cole said.

"Time to bail." Mack parked along the side of the street. The team got out and ran the remaining five blocks to the hotel.

By the time they got near, the police were setting up barricades across the road. Fire trucks and law-enforcement vehicles made it impossible for any other vehicles to access the hotel.

Guests streamed out of the hotel dressed in their finest. Men in black suits, wired with radio headsets, scurried around the entrances. Secret Service.

Cole stopped a man and woman walking away from the hotel. "What's going on?" he asked, knowing for the most part why they'd been evacuated.

"Someone called in a bomb threat. They've evacuated the entire building."

The woman shivered in the cool night air. "They wouldn't even let us get our coats."

"Did they get the president out?" Cole asked.

The man frowned. "The Secret Service gathered him and the vice president and took them out of the ballroom through the rear exit. I'm sure the president is back at the White House by now, sitting in front of a fireplace keeping warm. Unlike the rest of us." He draped his arm around the woman's shoulders and pulled her close. "Come on, we'll find a cab a couple blocks away from this nightmare."

"I can't walk too far in these shoes," she complained as they continued away from the hotel. "I wasn't expecting to hike in this outfit."

"What if they didn't get the president out of the hotel?" CJ said.

"We don't know how they plan to kill the president. It could be with explosives or they might plan on a sniper taking him out as he leaves."

"Carpenter said they would eliminate Charlie

as well as the president," Mack said. "How would they do that and spare the others?"

Cole swore. "I might have made it that much easier for them by calling in the bomb threat."

"How are we going to get in?" Mack asked.

"Come on," Cole said. "I have an idea." Weaving through the crowd leaving the hotel, they found an ambulance parked near the entrance, a stretcher unfolded and ready for anyone who might need assistance. An EMT had just climbed up into the back of the ambulance for supplies, leaving the stretcher unattended.

Cole grabbed the stretcher and rolled it past a police car. "Mack, get the other end," he said. CJ swiped the EMT's tool kit and hurried after them.

With Cole walking backward and Mack pushing the other end, they walked right past the police but were stopped by the Secret Service men guarding the front of the building.

"We were told Charlotte Halverson is in need of medical support. Please, step aside," Cole said.

"We can't let you inside," the man in the black suit said.

"Mrs. Halverson funds half the hospitals in the DC area," Cole said. "Do you want to be responsible for her death and the cessation of funding to those hospitals?"

The man stood tall, his chest puffed out, a rifle in his arms. "Can't let you in."

"Very well," Cole said. "Let it be on your shoulders when she dies."

"Oh, dear Lord," CJ jerked and clutched her shoulder. "I've been hit!" She dropped to the ground and moaned. "They're shooting at us. I've been hit."

The agent crouched and looked up at the buildings surrounding them. "Get down!" he called out. Everyone within earshot ducked. Women dressed in evening gowns screamed and dropped to their knees.

In the confusion, the five Defenders slipped past the guards, entered the hotel, sidestepped the metal detectors and kept moving, following the signs leading to the ballroom. The first chance they got, they ditched the gurney.

Cole didn't like leaving CJ outside the hotel, but knew they had to get to Charlie and the president.

"CJ? Are you okay?"

For a moment, he thought their headsets had quit working. But then he heard the soft sound of her voice,

"I'm okay. I'll see you inside."

"Don't try. We'll take care of this."

A bad feeling hit Cole in the pit of his belly. What were the chances that CJ would stay put outside the hotel?

Slim to none.

If Trinity had its people inside and they ran into CJ, they'd take her out, as well.

Damn.

Cole fought the urge to turn around and run back out to the front of the hotel. They had a job to do. The fate of the nation and Declan's Defenders rode on the outcome.

Secret Service agents combed the ballroom. Several had bomb-sniffing dogs, checking every square inch of the room.

Cole stopped one of the agents. "Did they get the president out?"

The agent frowned. "Of course. Who the hell are you and how did you get in?"

"We're from the bomb squad," Cole lied. "We're here to defuse the bomb when you find it."

"Good. I'd like to keep all my parts in place." The agent nodded toward the rear of the ballroom. "They took POTUS and the VP out that way, along with that billionaire philanthropist, Halverson, and some guy." He shrugged. "Not sure why they took her. Maybe the president wants her to fund his next election campaign."

"Why that way and not out the front?" Cole asked.

"They have several escape plans for each event the president attends. Going out the front, going out the back and going up. If they go up, they have to hold until Marine One can get here. If the helo can't land on the roof, they'll call for a Navy SEAL team to extract them."

"We'll be around if you find anything," Cole said. "All you have to do is yell."

"Don't go far. If a clock is ticking, we might be on borrowed time," the agent said. He went back to work searching under chairs and tables draped in fancy white linens, set with gold charger plates and crystal glasses and candelabras.

A man in a black suit was on a ladder in the middle of the room, checking out the huge crystal chandelier.

Cole, Mack, Mustang, Jack and Gus moved through the room to the rear exit. Mack pulled out his cell phone.

"Calling Declan?" Cole asked as they pushed through the double doors into a hallway.

Mack nodded. "I don't know why they're not answering. If they were evacuated, they'd have been outside by now."

"Try Arnold," Cole said. "He was Charlie's date."

Mack dialed the butler's number.

A moment later, he looked up. "Nothing."

Then his phone pinged. Mack stared down at the screen. "It's a text from Declan."

The men gathered around Mack.

Head for the top. Trinity has POTUS, VP, Roger and Charlie. Take stairs.

"They're headed for the roof," Cole said. "Find the stairs."

AFTER CJ FAKED being shot and had everyone ducking to avoid being hit, she rolled away from the guard at the door and ducked into the building following another Secret Service agent. She dodged the metal detectors to avoid setting off an alarm with the gun she had stashed beneath the jacket she wore that was splattered in her own blood.

She'd listened to the one-sided conversation she could hear as Cole spoke with someone about them being part of the bomb squad. She chuckled as she headed down a hallway. When she heard them talk about the text from Declan and needing to get to the roof, she found a stairwell and started up. She ran, though her ankle hurt and her shoulder throbbed. They were the least of her worries. Charlie was in trouble. And Trinity was planning to kill the president and possibly the vice president.

If they both died, the speaker of the house was next in line for the presidency. Had the speaker of the house been the leader of Trinity all along? CJ thought about who that was and shook her head. The speaker of the house was a man who had been married to the same woman for thirty years, had two beautiful daughters and five grandchildren. He went to church on Sundays and volunteered at children's hospitals in his home state and in the DC area. He couldn't be the Trinity leader.

And the vice president had been kidnapped by Trinity along with Anne Bellamy just a little while ago, a plot foiled by the Declan crew. Trinity wouldn't kidnap their own leader, would they?

Unless they wanted to throw others off. Who would believe they would kidnap their own leader? No one. But they hadn't killed him when they could have. They'd used the VP and Anne Bellamy to lure CJ out of hiding.

They'd succeeded in that effort. CJ wasn't hiding anymore. But they hadn't been quick enough to kill her. She'd stayed one step ahead. With the help of Declan's Defenders, she'd gotten that much closer to learning who was in charge of Trinity.

She'd hoped that when she'd discovered Chris Carpenter in the main house on the compound, that he would prove to be their leader. But he'd been pretty confident that Trinity would have someone in the highest office in the US soon. Since he wasn't with the president at the time, nor in position to take over the presidency, he clearly wasn't the guy.

Which brought it down to one of two people. The vice president and the speaker of the house.

CJ's money was on the vice president. The sooner she got to them, the sooner she'd find out.

Taking the stairs two at a time, she ignored the pain in her ankle and in her shoulder and powered through, climbing the eight stories to the top, her breath fast and heavy. When she reached the eighth floor, she found a smaller stairwell with a locked gate in front of it. A sign read Authorized Personnel Only.

CJ vaulted over the gate, landing on the first stair leading upward. Since she hadn't heard anyone in the stairwell or seen the others of her group, she assumed they were climbing a different set of steps to the roof. She hoped they arrived around the same time as she did. They'd all need backup.

If it was true the Secret Service had evacuated the POTUS, VP and Charlie, they were probably Trinity sleeper agents who'd managed to get past the background checks to become Secret Service staff members. They'd be highly trained as assassins as well as having gone through specialized training for the Secret Service. They'd be formidable foes in hand-to-hand or weapon fights.

When CJ reached the top of the stairs, the door led out onto the rooftop of the hotel. A rectangular window allowed her to peer through before she made her move to step out onto the roof.

As far as she could see, there were air-conditioning units jutting out of the roof near her end of the long, rectangular building. A structure graced the other end of the building. It appeared to be a rooftop bar with large windows on the side she could see. Outside the windows, there was a patio area with tables, chairs and potted plants in large concrete containers. Based on the direction the bar faced, it had a view of the city customers would pay top dollar to admire.

"Declan just texted." Cole's voice sounded in her earbud headset and made her feel warm all over. "They're in the rooftop bar. He can see them through the window. The men dressed as Secret Service are holding the president, Charlie and Roger hostage."

"What about the vice president?" one of the guys asked.

CJ waited, her heart pounding, hanging on the edge, eager to hear Cole again.

Cole swore. "He's calling the shots."

CJ nodded. As she suspected. Vice President Gordon Helms would be next in command should the president die. He'd be the leader of the US until the next election.

"That's our guy. The bastard we've been searching for," Gus said in his gruff voice. "How many guns?"

Another pause before Cole answered. "Six men in black. And the VP is carrying."

Six. The trick would be to get inside the bar without being detected.

If they made too daring a move, Trinity would push the process forward and kill the president, Charlie and Roger before they had a chance to rescue them.

"How do we want to handle this?"

"None of us was able to bring in the rifles. All we have are small arms. We can't pick them off without several sniper rifles going at the same time." It was Mack's voice. "We have to get inside or get close enough to shoot through the glass."

"There are planters, tables with umbrellas, and chairs on a patio close to me," CJ interjected. "I can low-crawl to within a few feet of the windows."

"It's too dangerous," Cole said.

"I can do it," CJ insisted. "Going now. I'll let you know when I'm in position."

"CJ," Cole said.

She ignored him and slipped out of the door onto the roof. Keeping low, she moved in the shadows of the AC units until she reached the edge of the patio, partitioned off by a wrought-iron railing. CJ crept alongside the building where there were no windows and rolled over the top of the railing, landing on the patio. She lay still, listening for movement from inside. When she thought all was quiet, she low crawled on her belly, moving from the cover of a giant pot to the shadow of a table to another giant pot until she was close enough she could see through the windows to the people gathered around.

Her heart caught in her throat when she located Charlie. The older woman sat on the floor beside a body of a man in a tuxedo. His head lay across her lap and she held his hand.

Roger Arnold, the butler.

Charlie raised his hand to her cheek and held it there.

Was he dead?

The butler brushed his knuckles across her cheek and his lips moved.

CJ let go of the breath she'd been holding. "I can see the six men dressed as Secret Service agents, the vice president, Charlie, Arnold and the president. I have ten rounds in my gun. I can take them out, but not all at once."

"Wait until we get in position on the other side," Cole said.

From where she was, CJ could see that the patio extended around the front of the bar to the other side with a similar setup of tables with umbrellas, chairs and potted plants.

"Gus and Mack met up with Declan. They're going in through the back door once the war begins," Cole said. "Jack, Mustang and I can take out the four men close to the vice president."

"I can take the other two who are closer to my side of the bar," CJ said.

"What if they're not Trinity?" Jack asked. "What if they're really there to protect the VP and president?"

The vice president lifted his weapon and fired at one of the men in black. The man dropped where he stood. The others didn't flinch.

"I'd say that answers our question," CJ said.

"On three," Cole said. "One."

CJ positioned herself, holding her Glock steady with one hand braced beneath the handle.

"Two."

The vice president waved his gun at one of the men in black.

That man raised his weapon and aimed it at Charlie.

"He's going to shoot Charlie," CJ said, and fired on the guy.

Chapter Thirteen

CJ's bullet pierced the window with a clean, round hole and hit her target in the side of his head. He fell to the ground.

The president sank to the floor beside Charlie and Arnold, out of range of the bullets flying over their heads.

Cole and Jack dropped their men and CJ hit the second guy on her side in a clean kill, taking him down with a bullet through the chest.

That left the vice president as the only man holding a gun still alive.

Gus, Declan and Mack burst through the back door into the bar, their weapons leveled on Helms, but a second too late.

Helms had grabbed the president from behind and pressed his gun against the man's temple. Through the holes in the windows, CJ heard the VP say, "Drop your weapons or I'll shoot him."

CJ leaped to her feet and raced for the back

door, coming to a skidding halt beside Mack and Gus. "If you drop your weapons," CJ said, "he'll shoot the president anyway, then he'll shoot you. That's what Trinity does. Isn't that right, Director?"

"I don't know what you're talking about," Helms said. "You worked for Trinity. You should know."

"He shot Roger," Charlie said, her lips pulled back in a sneer. "He told one of the men to shoot me."

"Shut up, woman," Helms yelled. "Or I'll shoot you myself." He jerked his head toward Mack. "Now, are you going to put your weapons down, or am I going to put a bullet in the head of your commander in chief?"

"You might as well give up now," CJ said. "Carpenter is dead. His wife and the Russian are dead. The compound is burned to the ground and your thugs are dead. You'll be sad to know your plan to burn the kids in the dorms didn't work. We got all of them out before we lost even one."

Movement from the floor caught CJ's attention.

Roger Arnold, Charlie's butler and former SAS soldier, lunged for Helms, knocking the gun away from the president's temple and up toward the ceiling.

Helms pulled the trigger. The bullet went wide, lodging somewhere in the ceiling.

Roger fell to the floor, spent.

Helms raised his weapon and aimed it at CJ.

Before he could fire, three bullets hit him, one each from Gus, Mack and CJ's guns, sending him staggering backward with each impact.

Still, he raised his weapon and aimed again at CJ.

A shot was fired from beside CJ, hitting Helms in the head. The man dropped and lay completely still.

CJ turned to find Cole standing beside her.

"Took you long enough to get here," she quipped and fell into his arms.

"I thought you had it all under control," he said, holding her close, his strong arms surrounding her.

She didn't care if she looked weak or like she couldn't handle one more Trinity agent. CJ was in Cole's arms and she liked it there.

COLE WAS GLAD to hold her. He'd gone through all kinds of hell worrying about her when she'd been out of his sight. And then to walk into the bar and see the vice president aiming his gun at her... He'd done the only thing he could do and shot the man in the head.

Declan reached a hand down to help Charlie to her feet.

She waved his hand away and scooted across

the floor in her long gown to brush a hand across Roger Arnold's forehead. "My hero," she murmured.

"Mine, too," said the president. He rose to his feet, straightened his suit jacket and stood tall. "I don't know who you men are, but I owe you my life."

Declan straightened and, wincing, pressed a hand to his midsection. "These are my team of Declan's Defenders. I'm Declan O'Neill. This is Mack Balkman, my second in command."

Mack raised a hand.

Declan pointed to Mustang. "He's Frank 'Mustang' Ford."

Mustang nodded.

Declan waved a hand toward Gus. "Gus Walsh."

"Sir," Gus said, coming to attention.

Pointing to Cole, Declan said, "Cole McCastlain."

"Pleasure to meet you, Mr. President," Cole said without loosening his hold on CJ.

Declan pointed to Jack. "Our slack man is Jack Snow. The youngest man on the team."

Jack popped a salute. "It's an honor, sir!"

The president's eyes narrowed. "Prior military?"

"Yes, sir," Declan responded. "Marine Force Recon."

"The best of the best," the president murmured. "I take it you're not in the marines anymore?"

Declan's lips thinned. "No, sir."

The president's brow furrowed. "I'd like to know why."

"Sir, it's a long story," Cole said. "And some of these folks need medical attention." He looked down at CJ. "No argument."

"And this young lady is?" The president held out his hand to CJ.

"Nobody you need to concern yourself with," CJ answered, afraid she'd be arrested if anyone were to recall that Helms had just revealed she'd once been a part of the same organization that had just attempted to assassinate the president.

"You saved my life," the president said. "I'd say that you are well worth getting to know."

CJ couldn't ignore the man's hand and shook it.

"Thank you for coming to my rescue," the president said, his tone deep and sincere.

"You're welcome, sir," CJ responded, her face suffusing with color.

"Are you blushing?" Cole whispered close to her ear.

She elbowed him in the side. "No."

He chuckled softly. "Liar."

"Mrs. Halverson." The president turned to Charlie.

"Please, sir, call me Charlie," she said with a smile.

"Your date had a major role in saving my life, as well. I'd like to get to know him better."

"Sir," Arnold said in his mild English accent, from his position lying on the floor. "Roger Arnold, the Queen's SAS, at your service. Pardon me if I don't rise. I seem to have caught a bullet."

Mack removed a headset from one of the dead Trinity gunmen who'd been undercover as a Secret Service agent and tapped into the radio frequency for the president's men. "We need medical assistance in the rooftop bar. And send more men up to guard the president."

"I think I'm better off with you gentlemen as my bodyguards," the president said. "Where does one hire such men?"

Declan turned to Charlie. "Sir, you'll have to go through our boss. Charlie's the one who had the idea to pull this team together. She deserves the credit."

"Far from it," Charlie said. "I only tapped on some talent the Marine Corps let slip through its fingers. When you get a moment when your life is no longer in danger, Mr. President, I'd like to have a meeting with you on that very subject."

"I'll be sure to have my people put you on my schedule. Would you like to meet at my place or yours?"

Charlie laughed. "Yours, of course. You travel with far too much baggage." She winked and took Arnold's hand in hers. "I'll have my people get with your people to make it happen."

"Yes, ma'am," the president said with a smile.

The Secret Service men swarmed in on the bar and surrounded the president, hustling him out of the bar and hotel, and into a waiting limousine.

Charlie, CJ and the team waited for emergency medical technicians to arrive and lift Arnold onto the stretcher that was probably the one they'd appropriated to help them get past the guards what felt like hours before.

When Arnold had been loaded into the ambulance, Charlie insisted on going with him. Declan joined them, adamant that someone needed to provide for Charlie's protection. Based on the blood seeping through his shirt, he needed the trip to the hospital for a recheck on his gunshot wound.

Cole insisted CJ also go to the hospital. She refused.

"Charlie has a doctor who will make house calls," Mack said. "Let's get her back to Charlie's place."

Mack and Mustang hurried out to where the team had left the SUV parked several blocks away and drove back to collect the other Defenders and CJ.

By the time they'd returned, the blockades had

been cleared and they were able to drive up to the front of the hotel.

Tired and dirty, Cole wanted nothing more than to climb into a shower with CJ and then lie in bed with her in his arms, making love until they both fell asleep from sheer exhaustion.

CJ sat silently beside him, all the way to Charlie's estate.

Cole couldn't believe it was over and CJ was alive. They'd helped rid the world of the Director in charge of Trinity, the man who'd tried to ruin her life and that of so many others. Along with the burning of the training compound, Trinity would surely crumble.

When they reached the estate, Grace met them on the steps of the mansion.

"Charlie called to say CJ was hurt," Grace said. She hurried down to her. "The doctor is in the sitting room. He'll take care of you. If it's serious enough for surgery, we'll get you to a hospital ASAP."

"It's only a flesh wound," CJ insisted as they entered the foyer.

Cole's jaw tightened. "That's what Declan said. He's just lucky the bullet didn't hit any of his internal organs." He held up a hand when Grace shot a worried look in his direction. "Declan rode with the ambulance to provide protection for Charlie and Arnold. He'll have the ER doctor do a double check on his own injuries. And, no, he didn't sustain any more injuries tonight."

"If you think you can handle things here," Grace said, "I'd like to go to the hospital and be with Charlie, Roger and Declan."

"Go," CJ said. "I'll be fine."

Grace squeezed her hand and ran out the front door.

"I'd rather just get a shower and something to eat," CJ said, dragging her feet across the foyer.

Cole shook his head. "You're seeing the doctor. He'll determine how badly you're injured."

"Does anyone know what happened to all the kids from the compound?" CJ asked as Cole led her into the sitting room.

Jonah appeared in the hallway, coming out of the study. "They've been taken to a church's gymnasium for now until they can all be identified and cross-referenced against the missing or exploited children's database. Charlie had offered to set up a commission to handle the children."

"I'd like to be part of helping them through the repatriation process," CJ said.

"Later," Cole insisted. "You're having your shoulder examined right now."

"I know, but—" CJ started.

"But nothing," Cole grabbed the elbow of her good arm and marched her into the sitting room.

The doctor asked her to take a seat on a small ottoman.

Cole helped her remove her bloodstained jacket and shirt. The fabric stuck to her skin with the dried blood.

"I'll get a damp cloth," Cole said as he hurried out of the room.

Mack met him in the hallway with a towel, a bucket of warm water and a washcloth. "Thought she might need these."

Cole threw the towel over his shoulder. "Thanks."

Mack lifted his chin toward the sitting room. "Is she going to be all right?"

"Haven't got to the wound yet." Cole took the bucket and the washcloth. "I'll let you know."

"She was pretty amazing tonight," Mack said as he released the handle of the bucket.

Cole's chest tightened. CJ was everything. Skilled at warfare, a great shooter, tough, tender and had a heart buried deep in all that Trinity training. "Tell me about it."

"I don't know what's going on between you two, but she's a keeper. She could probably do better, but you can't." Mack grinned and clapped a hand on Cole's shoulder. "Be nice and she might stick around."

Cole walked back into the sitting room, mulling over what Mack had said.

The doctor draped the towel around CJ and

used the washcloth and warm water to wet the fabric stuck in dried blood. Before long, the water did the trick and he was able to ease the fabric away from the wound and remove the shirt altogether. She sat in a white lace bra, completely at ease with her body and the fact that she was in the presence of two men in only her underwear.

Cole smiled. Tough and confident. That was CJ.

Once he had the wound cleaned, the doctor could better see how bad it was. "You're lucky. It doesn't appear to have damaged any muscle tissue," he said. After applying a local anesthetic around the gash, he removed the bullet and sutured the skin together with three small stitches. "You'll be fine, as long as you keep it clean and watch for infection. I'll be back to take the stitches out at the end of next week."

CJ nodded. "Thanks." Then she draped the damp towel over her shoulders. "Any problem with showering? I'd like to wash the rest of the dirt and soot from my body."

"No problem at all. Once you're done, apply this antibiotic cream to the wound and cover it in gauze and tape." He pulled out the supplies she'd need and gave her instructions on the care and cleaning of the wound for the next week. "If you suspect it's getting infected, don't wait, call me. I'll be back out."

Cole and CJ walked the doctor to the door.

"Not many doctors perform house calls anymore," Cole remarked. "Thank you for making the effort."

The doctor shook his head. "I would do anything for Charlie. She's done so much for me." He shook hands with Cole and CJ and then left.

"Seems Charlie has a fan club," CJ remarked as she headed for the stairs.

Cole followed. "The woman has saved so many lives through her generosity."

CJ glanced up at him as they climbed the staircase side by side. "Like yours and all of Declan's Defenders'?"

He nodded. "When we were dishonorably discharged, no one would hire us. And what skills did we bring to the table? Who wanted combat-trained men in their factories or businesses?"

CJ nodded. "I face the same situation, only worse. My résumé would read 'trained assassin.' The only people who are going to hire me are men wanting to off their wives to collect insurance money or to keep them from having to pay alimony or half their fortunes to an ex." She snorted. "I'm done with killing. I'd rather spend my time helping the children Trinity recruited to reclaim their childhoods before they become like me."

They were at the top of the stairs when Cole turned CJ to face him. "They'd be lucky to become like you. You're amazingly strong, both physically and here—" he touched a finger to her chest "—where it counts most. Even though Trinity tried to brainwash you into becoming a killing machine, you knew, deep down, right from wrong and fought for what you believed. That took more chutzpah than toeing the Trinity line and completing their list of hits."

He tipped her chin up and brushed at the line of soot smeared across her cheek. "You're beautiful inside and out." He bent to touch his lips to hers. "I wouldn't want you any other way."

She pushed up on her toes to meet his mouth, returning the pressure in a kiss as gentle as it was passionate.

When they broke apart, CJ laughed. "Look at us, all filthy when there's a shower not ten feet away." She took his hand and led him down the hall to the bathroom.

Once inside, she shut the door and pushed the jacket from his shoulders. It dropped to the ground, sending up a waft of soot to sting their noses.

Cole removed the towel from her shoulders and let it slide to the floor to join his jacket. Then he helped her out of her leggings and shoes until she stood there in her panties and bra.

"Before we go any further, I have one question for you."

Her brow furrowed. "And what's that?" she said, reaching for the button on his jeans.

"What does CJ stand for?"

She laughed. "We've made love and you don't know?"

He shrugged. "Always seemed to get pushed to the back of my mind when I had other things to concentrate on. But now, I don't want to go any further until I know just who I'm making love to." He covered her hands with his before she could lower his zipper.

She looked up at him with a twisted grin. "It's not nearly as intimidating as the initials."

"I'm not looking to be intimidated." His fingers squeezed hers. "Tell me."

"I haven't been called by my given name since I was turned over to child protective services and placed in foster care. Right before Trinity stole me away from the home in which I'd been assigned."

He kissed her forehead. "You're stalling." Trailing kisses from her temple, across her cheek to her mouth, he paused. "Tell me."

"We need showers," she whispered. "How can you kiss me when I'm so dirty?"

"I like you dirty," he said and brushed her lips with his.

When she rose up again on her toes, he lifted his head. "Uh-uh. Not until you tell me."

CJ dropped back on her heels. "It's no big deal."

He let go of her and crossed his arms over his chest. "I'm waiting."

"Fine." CJ looked away. "My given name is Cara Jo Grainger. I go by CJ because Cara Jo sounds too soft and girlie."

"Cara Jo." Cole grinned.

CJ swung at him. "See? It's not me."

Cole pulled her into his arms and tipped her chin upward with a finger. "It's most definitely you. Because, you see, you might be the hard-as-nails CJ to everyone else, but I know beneath that outer shell is the soft Cara Jo, fighting to get out."

"I'm not soft," CJ said. "And I'm going for that shower, even if you aren't." She stepped out of his embrace, her panties and bra, and into the shower stall. The water switched on and she leaned out, a frown denting her pretty brow. "Are you coming?"

Cole didn't need a second invitation. He stripped off his shirt, jeans and shoes and stepped into the shower with her.

Half an hour later, the water had chilled, but their passion had not.

Cole gently dried Cara and wrapped her in a big, fluffy towel. He dried himself and looped a towel around his waist. Following the doctor's instructions, he applied the ointment to her wound and dressed it in the gauze and medical tape. Then he scooped her up into his arms and carried her across the hall into his bedroom and made love to her into the night, careful not to jar her, or cause her any pain. When they'd spent themselves, he lay beside her and slept the sleep of the sexually satisfied and thoroughly exhausted, knowing that when he woke, Cara would be beside him.

CJ SLEPT HARD for the first time in years, waking early before Cole stirred. For a long time, she lay on her side, staring at the man who'd been beside her, relentlessly looking out for her well-being and safety.

With the Director dead and the training camp burned to the ground, Trinity had lost its strength. But there were agents out there now who didn't have leadership or anyone to guide them. What would they do now that they were basically out of a job?

She'd struggled over the past year to find herself without Trinity. Job applications were difficult when she couldn't list a single skill that applied to being a clerk in a doctor's office or pass the background check for many positions in the DC area.

Had she used her real name, a background check could have done one of two things. First, it could have alerted authorities that she was a cold case of a missing child. Second, a Trinity sleeper agent embedded in whatever government office processing the background check could have found her. They would have eliminated her before she'd had the chance to save Anne Bellamy and the man she'd thought was a trustworthy vice president.

Now that Trinity was defunct, Cole wouldn't need to protect her. She could move out of Charlie's house and start all over somewhere safe. A place that would allow her to be anything she wanted. As long as she had a new identity. From what she'd seen Jonah was capable of, he could set her up with that new identity.

CJ rolled out of the bed, wrapped the towel around herself and crept into her room, where she dug into her backpack for her clothes and dressed quickly.

Once dressed, she headed down to the war room where she found Jonah at his computer.

"Do you ever sleep?" she asked.

"Good morning, Ms. Grainger." Jonah glanced up briefly with a smile. "I'll have you know that I slept like a baby last night." He went back to tapping on the keyboard. "Knowing the Director was taken care of and the man who'd killed Mr. Halverson was dead cleared my mind for the first time since John Halverson's death." Jonah's hands paused on the keyboard. "He was a good man."

"I wish I'd known him. Seems he had a way with bringing people together," CJ said.

"He had a way of giving people a second chance. I was a snot-nosed kid hacking into bank accounts when he found me about to be caught by the Feds. He pulled me into his home and gave me a place to live. Hell, he made me part of his family. I loved him like the father I never knew. And Charlie…she's been there for me. I'd do anything for them."

CJ held up her hands. "I believe you. Charlie's amazing, and the team she hired has been nothing but professional and competent."

Jonah nodded and turned to CJ. "What brings you to the war room so early this morning? I know it's not to hear about me or how I came to be living on the Halverson estate."

"No, but I'm glad you told me. I'm glad to know I'm not the only stray Charlie has taken in. She's got a good heart." She paused briefly before adding, "I need a new identity. A chance to start my life over."

Jonah nodded. "I can help you with that. Like I helped Jane Doe—I mean Jasmine Newman." He cracked his knuckles and turned back to his computer. "Who do you want to be? A teacher? A physicist? A police officer?"

"I want to be someone who helps children like those who were recruited into Trinity. I don't want what happened to me to happen to them."

"I can make you a social worker with a degree and everything."

CJ shook her head. "No, Jonah. I want you to give my life back to me. I want to be Cara Jo

Grainger. But I don't want to be on anyone's database as having been a missing child or having been a part of Trinity. I want to go to college, get a degree and learn how to go about helping others. I just want to be me. Cara Jo Grainger."

Jonah turned to her and nodded. "I can help you with the database part, but you're going to have to find your way back to that person on your own. Trust me. I know. I've been there and I'm glad I don't have to do that again. And you can't go back and reclaim what you lost. You have to move forward and become the person you want to be." He stood and held out his hand. "We can start right now. Hi, I'm Jonah Spradlin. Pleased to meet you."

She smiled and took the younger man's hand. "I'm Cara Jo Grainger. The pleasure's mine." Then she pulled Jonah into a hug and let the tears slide down her cheeks. "Thank you, Jonah."

"Hey, what's going on here?" Cole's voice sounded behind them.

Jonah stood back and waved a hand at CJ. "Cole McCastlain, I'd like to introduce you to Cara Jo Grainger. She's new in town. I hear she's good with kids and she has a heart of gold."

Cole's brow furrowed and his eyes narrowed, but he went along with the introduction. "Miss Grainger, I'm pleased to meet you." He held out his hand.

CJ placed her hand in his. When his warm fingers curled around hers, she felt the electric current running between them. "Please. Call me Cara Jo."

"Cara Jo," Cole said. Then he pulled her into his arms and hugged her close.

"I'm ready," she said into his chest.

"Ready for what?" he asked.

"Ready to start over." She looked up into his eyes. "It's not too late, is it?"

"No, babe, it's not too late." He kissed the tip of her nose. "Just do me one favor."

"Name it," she said.

"Don't change who you are," he whispered.

CJ frowned. "But I can't be the CJ of the past."

He shook his head. "You'll always be the CJ of your past. It's what made you the kind, caring, incredibly strong woman you are today." He brushed his lips across hers. "It makes you the woman I'm falling in love with. The woman I don't want to let go of…for the rest of my life."

Her heart skipped several beats and then raced, pushing blood through her veins so fast she thought they might burst. "How could you fall in love with me? I'm a trained assassin." She had to admit to herself that his words of love were like a dream come true, but how could they be real? She didn't deserve his love. She'd killed people.

"Your past doesn't dictate your future. But it

helps to shape you into the woman you want to become." He brushed a thumb across her damp cheek. "From where I'm standing, you're pretty awesome already. I want to be with you as you rebuild your life and you improve on the woman you already are."

"Mr. McCastlain, I don't think you know what you're getting yourself into."

"Oh, sweetheart, I know, and I can't wait to see what new adventures we'll come up with next."

She rested her hands on his chest where his heart beat strong and his muscles flexed when he moved. With a twisted smile, she stared up into his eyes. "Then hold on to your hat, cowboy. It's going to be a helluva ride."

Chapter Fourteen

Cole grabbed two longnecks out of the ice chest on the covered patio overlooking the pool at Charlie Halverson's mansion. After opening them, he handed one to Declan and the other to Mack.

"Aren't you having one for yourself?" Mack asked.

Cole shook his head. "No, thank you. I'm swearing off alcohol for the time being," he said and patted his midsection. "The older you get, the more weight you gain. I don't plan on developing a beer belly."

Mack drank half the bottle before he set it on the table in front of him. "Can I get you another rum and Coke?" he asked Riley Lansing, who sat in the seat beside him. He'd been holding her hand for the past hour as they sat staring out at the rippling water of the backyard pool and Charlie's rose garden, chatting with the rest of the team and their ladies.

"I can't believe it's been six months since I first met Declan, and he saved me from Trinity when they tried to kidnap me on Capitol Hill." Charlie leaned against Roger Arnold, an arm around his waist. "John would have been so proud of what you all have accomplished."

"What you've accomplished," Declan said, raising his bottle of beer to Charlie. "Had you not offered my team a job, none of it would have happened. Trinity would still be around and they could have had their leader as president."

Cole shook his head. "Our world could have been a very different place at this point in time. But, because you had faith in us, our presidency is safe, we have a new vice president who happens to be female, and the children of Trinity are learning how to be kids again."

"How's that going, Charlie?" Anne Bellamy asked from where she sat in the same lounge chair with Jack.

Charlie smiled. "Ask Cara Jo, she's been working as a volunteer since we set up the John Halverson Children's Foundation."

As all gazes turned to CJ, she smiled. "It's going to be a long road, but they're coming along better than expected. The discipline they learned from Trinity is coming in handy. Some of them have been rehomed in foster care. Others have chosen to remain in the foundation boarding school.

We've set up a sports program to keep them busy and out of temptation. Many of them are showing a lot of promise in academics."

"How's the course work coming, Cara Jo?" Declan asked.

CJ's chest puffed out. "I made the dean's list this semester."

Everyone congratulated her.

Cole slipped an arm around CJ and pulled her close. "I was so proud of her, I knew if I didn't do something soon, I might lose her forever."

"What are you talking about, man?" Mustang asked. "Cara Jo's not going anywhere. She's one of us."

CJ's joy bubbled over at the compliment. Being a part of the team meant the world to her. Almost as much as being a part of Cole's life. She held up her left hand. "You guys are stuck with me. Cole asked. I said yes. We're engaged!"

Riley, Anne, Emily Chastain, Jasmine and Grace rushed forward to admire the ring and hug the happy couple.

"Have you picked a date?" Grace asked.

Cole's cheeks turned a charming shade of red. "Actually, we're getting married really soon. I need you all to clear your calendars for the weekend after next."

A collective gasp was followed by the women

shaking their heads, and mentions of *impossible* and *that's crazy* were murmured.

Gus was the one to break through with the question everyone must have been wondering and one CJ was excited to answer. "Why so quick?"

Cole looked to CJ. "You want to tell them?"

She smiled and pressed a hand to her flat belly. "I'm pregnant. The baby is due in six months."

"So that's why you're not drinking alcohol?" Declan laughed. "I should have known something was up. You never pass on a good beer."

"As long as Cara Jo can't drink alcohol, I'm swearing off." Cole kissed CJ's temple. "We're in this together."

Mustang chuckled. "Sounds like you're going into battle."

Cole ran a hand through his hair. "Sometimes I think I'm going into battle without a weapon. What do I know about raising a kid?"

CJ hugged him around the middle. "As much as I do. Don't tell me you're scared, because that would make two of us."

Grace hugged CJ and then Cole. "You two will be just fine. And that baby will have the love of a dozen honorary aunts and uncles."

"You bet. And a cousin to play with," Declan said.

Grace glared at him. "Shh. This is CJ and Cole's moment."

Cole's eyes narrowed. "Wait. What is this about a cousin to play with?"

Mustang leaned forward as Cole's gaze pinned Declan. The stares of the rest of the team and the women fixed on him, as well.

Declan winced and held up his hands in surrender. "Sorry, Grace. I just couldn't help myself." A grin spread across his face and he pulled Grace into his lap. "We're pregnant, too. But I didn't give up beer." Grace elbowed him in the gut. "But I guess I will now that the cat's out of the bag."

Roger Arnold stepped forward and cleared his throat. "While we're all confessing to big changes, Charlotte and I would like to make a couple of announcements." He turned to Charlie. "My love, you have the floor."

Charlie stepped forward with a paper in her hand. "I have with me a letter from the president of the United States."

Everyone grew silent.

"As you all know, I've been to visit the president on a number of occasions over the past few months since Declan's Defenders saved his life. Out of those meetings, we came up with the foundation to help the children of Trinity."

CJ's heart warmed, remembering how Charlie had gone into high gear to find a building with a dormitory and classrooms to house the children who would otherwise have inundated the state of

Virginia's social services with too many children to place into foster homes. And with the need to teach them to think like regular kids, they were not good candidates to go straight into homes.

Charlie had spent millions of dollars to bring the facilities up to standard and make it more of a home than an institution for the children. CJ and the rest of the team—especially the women—had had a hand in helping paint, decorate and shop for everything they needed from clothing to toys and toothbrushes.

"I also made a special request to our commander in chief. I asked him to fix what was broken." She held up the paper and smiled. "Today, he came through. This letter confirms that each of my Declan's Defenders has had their military records expunged of the dishonorable discharge. You are all eligible to return to active duty and Marine Force Reconnaissance, if you so desire. The president says he would be honored if you would consider coming back to work for him and our country."

Declan stood, his eyes suspiciously shiny. "Seriously?" He paced the tiled patio, shoving his hand through his hair. "We're no longer listed as dishonorably discharged?"

Cole stood beside CJ, his hand tightening around her middle.

She knew how much being a member of the

elite Marine Force Reconnaissance team had meant to him and the others.

She looked up at him, her heart thudding against her ribs. Her world on the cusp of yet another change. "If you want to go back to the Marine Corps, go. I'll support your decision."

"But would you come with me?" he asked. "It would mean moving away from the foundation, your college, Charlie and Roger."

She laid a hand on his chest. "I'll go wherever you go. Our baby will know her father."

"His," Cole corrected absently. "I could go back into the corps." He looked at Declan and his other teammates.

They all appeared to be in a state of shock.

Charlie frowned and chuckled. "This is not exactly the response I expected."

Mustang stood. "Charlie, don't get us wrong, we're thankful. It was a huge blow to us to be ejected from the corps we loved and swore our loyalty to."

"And worse, having the stigma of a dishonorable discharge on our records," Declan continued. "Having that expunged is a blessing."

Jack stepped forward, holding Anne's hand in his. "As much as we loved being a part of the military, of serving our country—" he looked around at the others "—we've loved being a part of Declan's Defenders." He frowned. "But maybe I'm speaking for myself, not the others."

"Snow's right," Cole said. "I didn't know how I would fit back into society after leaving the military. Who would ever need a man who knew how to fire a military rifle or a grenade launcher, or could drop a man at four hundred yards?" Cole shook his head. "I don't know about the others, but I was lost."

Mustang, Declan, Jack, Gus and Mack all nodded.

"If it weren't for Charlie, we might not still be together."

"Or we might have been statistics, like so many other guys who get off active duty and can't find their way home."

Silence settled over the men and women gathered at the Halverson estate.

CJ knew the statistics. Every day, twenty-two veterans took their lives. She couldn't imagine any of Declan's Defenders sinking to that level of desperation. They all seemed so confident and... happy. She pressed one hand to her belly, slid the other around Cole's waist and asked the question she wasn't sure she wanted to know the answer to. "So, what's it to be? Are you going to gather your team and report back to active duty?"

Declan pulled Grace up against his side. "What do you want me to do?"

Grace smiled up at him. "I want you to do what makes you happy."

"You'd follow me around the world?"

She nodded. "The baby and I will follow you wherever you go. We're part of your team now."

Declan kissed her and looked across the patio at his boss. "Charlie, if you still feel you need me, I'd be proud to serve on Declan's Defenders."

Charlie nodded. "Declan's Defenders has proved to be a viable and necessary organization. I'd be honored to have any and all of you continue to provide the service you've done so far."

Declan turned to his team. "If you feel the call to return to the corps, you need to do what is best for you. I'm staying."

Gus stepped forward. "So am I."

Mustang joined Gus. "Me, too."

Jack stepped up beside Declan. "I'm staying."

Mack slipped an arm around Riley. "I'm invested in the people here and the life we've begun. I'm staying."

Everyone turned to the last Defender. Cole.

"You're my brothers," Cole said. "Where you go, I go." He lifted his chin toward their benefactor. "And Charlie, Arnold and Jonah are family. I feel we found our way home when we came to work for you."

"Exactly," Declan agreed.

"But don't worry," Cole said. "We won't be

moving back in with you anytime soon. Seems you need to keep rooms open for the strays you manage to attract." He glanced down at CJ.

Her heart swelled with the love she'd found in this man. She knew she could live without him—she'd done it before—but he completed her like no one had done in her past.

"I love you, Cole McCastlain. And I love the life we're creating." She leaned up on her toes and pressed her lips to his.

Roger Arnold cleared his throat again. "Charlotte has another announcement to make, if you would be so good as to give her your attention once more." He smiled and nodded to Charlie.

Charlie's cheeks flushed with color. The woman looked young again and excited. "I have a job opening for a new butler."

CJ frowned. "Roger, you're not leaving us, are you?"

He shook his head but pressed his lips together and waited for Charlie to continue.

"No, Roger is not leaving us." She reached out a hand to him.

He took it and stepped up beside her, his shoulders thrown back, his head held high. "What Charlotte is saying is that she's agreed to become my wife."

Charlie's smile spread across her face. "I know it's only been ten months since my dear, sweet husband passed. Deep in my heart, I know he would approve of my decision. You see, Roger and John had been friends for a very long time. I think if I had met Roger first, I might have married him. But then, I loved John with all of my heart and I wouldn't have traded any day with him for the world.

"Roger came to me when I needed him most. After John was murdered. I don't know what I would have done without his support. But it's more than that." She turned to Roger, her eyes gleaming. "I love him as much, if not more than I loved John. Life has proven to be short. I'm not wasting another minute of it alone when I can be with the man I love." She turned to face them and held up her left hand. "Looks like we're going to have a few weddings in our near future."

CJ was the first to hug Charlie and Roger, her eyes filling with tears as she wished them all the happiness their hearts desired. Then she stepped back into Cole's arms and felt as if her world had come full circle.

She'd lost her family at a young age and wandered through life trying to fit in. Now she had a man who loved her, a group of friends who would give their lives to save hers and a baby on the way.

After all the years of loneliness, her world was full of love. Trinity had stolen her childhood, but she'd found her way home to Cole and his team.

Cole stood behind her, his arms around her, a hand spanning her belly. They had a life ahead of them and a child to love.

CJ leaned back against Cole and looked at him over her shoulder. "I love you, Cole."

"I love you, too, Cara Jo. You're everything I could have ever wanted and more." He kissed her temple. "And you're giving me the best gift of all."

"The baby?"

"Well, that, too. But I meant your love. I will treasure it, you and our children forever."

* * * * *

COMING NEXT MONTH FROM

◆ HARLEQUIN

INTRIGUE

Available February 18, 2020

#1911 BEFORE HE VANISHED
A Winchester, Tennessee Thriller • by Debra Webb
Halle Lane's best friend disappeared twenty-five years ago, but when
Liam Hart arrives in Winchester, Halle's certain he's the boy she once knew.
As the pair investigates Liam's mysterious past, can they uncover the truth
before a killer buries all evidence of the boy Halle once loved?

#1912 MYSTERIOUS ABDUCTION
A Badge of Honor Mystery • by Rita Herron
Cora Reeves's baby went missing in a fire five years ago, but she's convinced
the child is still out there. When Sheriff Jacob Maverick takes on the cold
case, new leads begin to appear—as well as new threats.

#1913 UNDERCOVER REBEL
The Mighty McKenzies Series • by Lena Diaz
Homeland Security agent Ian McKenzie has been working undercover
to break up a human-trafficking ring, but when things go sideways,
Shannon Murphy is suddenly caught in the crosshairs. Having only recently
learned the truth about Ian, can Shannon trust him with her life?

#1914 SOUTH DAKOTA SHOWDOWN
A Badlands Cops Novel • by Nicole Helm
Sheriff Jamison Wyatt has spent his life helping his loved ones escape his
father's ruthless gang. Yet when Liza Dean's sister finds herself caught in the
gang's most horrifying crime yet, they'll have to infiltrate the crime syndicate
and find her before it's too late.

#1915 PROTECTIVE OPERATION
A Stealth Novel • by Danica Winters
Shaye Geist and Chad Martin are both hiding from powerful enemies in the
wilds of Montana, and when they find an abandoned baby, they must join
forces. Can they keep themselves and the mysterious child safe—even as
enemies close in on all sides?

#1916 CRIMINAL ALLIANCE
Texas Brothers of Company B • by Angi Morgan
There's an algorithm that could destroy Dallas, and only FBI operative
Therese Ortis and Texas Ranger Wade Hamilton can find and stop it. But
going undercover is always dangerous. Can they accomplish their goal
before they're discovered? _____

**YOU CAN FIND MORE INFORMATION ON UPCOMING HARLEQUIN TITLES,
FREE EXCERPTS AND MORE AT HARLEQUIN.COM.**

HICNM0220

SPECIAL EXCERPT FROM

⬡HARLEQUIN
INTRIGUE

*Sheriff Jamison Wyatt has never forgotten Liza Dean,
the one who got away. But now she's back, and she needs
his help to find her sister. They'll have to infiltrate a crime
syndicate, but once they're on the inside, will they
be able to get back out?*

Read on for a sneak preview of
South Dakota Showdown *by Nicole Helm.*

Chapter One

Bonesteel, South Dakota, wasn't even a dot on most maps, which
was precisely why Jamison Wyatt enjoyed being its attached
officer. Though he was officially a deputy with the Valiant County
Sheriff's Department, as attached officer his patrol focused on
Bonesteel and its small number of residents.

One of six brothers, he wasn't the only Wyatt who acted as an
officer of the law—but he was the only man who'd signed up for
the job of protecting Bonesteel.

He'd grown up in the dangerous, unforgiving world of a biker
gang run by his father. The Sons of the Badlands were a cutthroat
group who'd been wreaking havoc on the small communities of
South Dakota—just like this one—for decades.

Luckily, Jamison had spent the first five years of his life on his
grandmother's ranch before his mother had fully given in to Ace
Wyatt and moved them into the fold of the nomadic biker gang.

Through tenacity and grit Jamison had held on to a belief in
right and wrong that his grandmother had instilled in him in those
early years. When his mother had given birth to son after son on the
inside of the Sons, Jamison had known he would get them out—
and he had, one by one—and escape to their grandmother's ranch
situated at the very edge of Valiant County.

It was Jamison's rough childhood in the gang and the immense responsibility he'd placed on himself to get his brothers away from it that had shaped him into a man who took everything perhaps a shade too seriously. Or so his brothers said.

Jamison had no regrets on that score. Seriousness kept people safe. He was old enough now to enjoy the relative quiet of patrolling a small town like Bonesteel. He had no desire to see lawbreaking. He'd seen enough. But he had a deep, abiding desire to make sure everything was right.

So it was odd to be faced with a clear B and E just a quarter past nine at night on the nearly deserted streets. Maybe if it had been the general store or gas station, he might have understood. But the figure was trying to break into his small office attached to city hall.

It was bold and ridiculous enough to be moderately amusing. Probably a drunk, he thought. Maybe the…woman—yes, it appeared to be a woman—was drunk and looking to sleep it off.

When he did get calls, they were often alcohol related and mostly harmless, as this appeared to be.

Since Jamison was finishing up his normal last patrol for the night, he was on foot. He walked slowly over, keeping his steps light and his body in the shadows. The streets were quiet, having long since been rolled up for the night.

Still, the woman worked on his doorknob. If she was drunk, she was awfully steady for one. Either way, she didn't look to pose much of a threat.

He stepped out of the shadow. "Typically people who break and enter are better at picking a lock."

The woman stopped what she was doing—but she hadn't jumped or shrieked or even stumbled. She just stilled.

Don't miss
South Dakota Showdown *by Nicole Helm,*
available March 2020 wherever
Harlequin Intrigue books and ebooks are sold.

Harlequin.com